A

Pirate's

Life

For Me

Untold

Secrets

By Daniel Addison

Chapter Art By
Ben Quinn –
Black Crow
Tattoo

Contents

Black Flag

Onboard they all muster,
Beneath moon covered lustre,
As they swear their allegiance
To a swashbuckling credence.
Set free from their past
As flag is tethered to mast,
Ready the Black Flag.

Through tempest of thunder,
They seek a new plunder.
Their captain draws sword
And points them toward
A ship in distance
With little resistance,
Raise the Black Flag.

On anchor does nestle
Their targeted vessel,
Tremendous in size
Yet not many to surprise.
They sail on closer
To pull up beside her,
Fly the Black Flag.

A sly trick from a soldier
As they're shoulder to shoulder,
Sleeping ship reawakens
With forces mistaken;
Their numbers increasing
And canons releasing,
Fight for the Black Flag.

No call for surrender
From a fearless contender,
The pirates give it their all
As each of them fall.
Captain lights the gunpowder
And sends both to fiery devour.
Die for the Black Flag.

History

Queen Anne's War began in 1702. The war waged between two factions; England and the Iroquois Confederacy against France and the Wabanaki Confederacy, which was fought on multiple fronts throughout Northern America. It was contemporaneous with the War of the Spanish Succession in Europe which involved a long list of divided countries, some of whom left their former allies The Bourbon Alliance and joined The Grand Alliance after a few years of the wars beginning.

The fighting throughout Europe and between the English and French North American Colonies had left off from unresolved conflicts of King William's War that ended in 1697.

The build-up began in November 1700 when the childless Spanish King Charles II, a member of the Hapsburg family, died and left the Monarchy of Spain to the grandson of King Louis XIV of France, a member of the rival Bourbon family. But William III of England had wanted the Holy

Roman Emperor, also a member of the Hapsburg family, to ascend to the Spanish throne instead, with the hopes that an alliance with the emperor would help England gain control of certain Spanish held locations in the Netherlands and Italy. He also believed that it disputed the lack of separation between the Spanish and French crowns, fearing that it threatened the European balance of power.

In March of 1702, William III died and

his sister-in-law, Anne, ascended to the English throne. A few months later, England joined the conflict when it declared war on Spain and France in May of 1702.

During the wars there was a heavy amount of sea warfare and the use of Privateers became very popular with both sides as they were usually unmarked ships that were privately owned and commissioned by a government to make reprisals, gain reparation from the crown for specific offenses in times of peace, or to prey upon the enemy in times of war.

No single event in history would change the face of privateering and piracy more than the Treaty of Utrecht in 1713, which ended the wars across Europe and Northern America. With the signing of the treaty, France ceded the Hudson Bay territory, Newfoundland, and Nova Scotia to Great Britain. France also agreed to a British protectorate over the Iroquois Indians. Spain recognised England's right to colonies in the New World and so Great Britain ceased attacks on Spanish ships. Almost overnight, English privateering was disbanded. The buccaneers were out of honest work and those who continued to attack Spanish commerce could be hanged as pirates instead of hailed as heroes.

Unfortunately for most of the privateers, there was no other work to turn to and so the obvious choice was to continue to do what they did best. Only now instead of giving a share to the crown, the former privateers kept their treasures to themselves and went to war with all nations. The once valiant hunters had become the hunted.

The Pirates had formed their own loose confederacy called The Republic of Pirates in Nassau, on New Providence Island in the Bahamas. It was governed by its own informal Code of Conduct which differed between reigning captains. They then began causing havoc throughout trade and shipping routes in the West Indies, attacking and plundering ships that crossed their paths.

After Queen Anne's death in 1714, parliament passes the Act of Settlement to ensure a Protestant succession as she had no heir to take her throne. She was succeeded by the German Protestant prince, George, Elector of Hanover.

King George took over the fight against pirates as their ranks began to strengthen and their unlawful activities intensified.

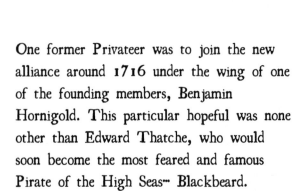

One former Privateer was to join the new alliance around 1716 under the wing of one of the founding members, Benjamin Hornigold. This particular hopeful was none other than Edward Thatche, who would soon become the most feared and famous Pirate of the High Seas~ Blackbeard.

(Illustration of Blackbeard from the 1724
Charles Johnson book *A General History of
the Robberies and Murders of the most
notorious Pyrates*)

Prologue

he undulating sound of the ocean echoes through the clouds in a mollifying harmonious sonata. The seagulls glide effortlessly amongst the salt air breeze, dipping and diving, weaving in and out of one another as they watch over curiously at the evolving mayhem below. The inquisitive birds swoop in closer to follow a returning ship as it enters a congested dockyard. As they break through the thick smoke trailing behind the distressed vessel and slalom through the singed, smoking vestiges of the masts, they are soon quick to change course and disperse back to the safety of the tranquil firmament as if haunted by the ghastly sights hidden within the smoldering wreckage.

The local townsfolk and traders look on
with troubled fixation as naval guards march
forward in angst to accost the battered
remains of a once proud military craft. Not
one they would have dismissed so easily
before, but one that they would have
formerly fought desperately over for a
position on board during its glorious
departure. Now they pick at the shattered
artistry and pull the lifeless, distorted bodies
of their lost colleagues from the embers, no
longer filled with passion and boisterous
arrogance but of a melancholic emptiness,
dreading their next orders from the
despairing hierarchy.

As the commotion continues, another
military ship is about to set sail for a
sacrificial assignment. The morose soldiers
shuffle their way slowly aboard like the
souls of the dead approaching the gates of
Hell as Hades welcomes them with a false
untruth of what lies ahead.
The preparations before sailing keep the
men busy, but every now and again they

catch a glimpse of the fragmented ship that
has already been to Purgatory and back,
demoralising their spirits further as they
continue their robotic directives.
However, one man seems unaltered by the
horrors surrounding him and pushing through
the queue of zombie soldiers he hurries to
the back of the ship in a frantic impatience
to see something for the last time.

Deep in the heart of town, a young boy
swings open his front door and yanks the
hand of his mother who is trying to keep
her balance as she puts on her shoes,
"Mother, come on! Father is leaving." He
squeals with excitement, oblivious to the
reality of what may happen to his father.
"Go ahead Jack, I'll be right behind you."
His mother demands emotionally, more
reluctant to leave the house than he is.
The boy releases his grip and rushes
through the bustling streets, dodging the
occasional bucket of human waste being
emptied out onto the unfortunate cobbles
from towering windows above and clambers
over the sick, drunk and homeless scattered

around the filthy pavement below. His determination leads him fearlessly through the crowds and the advantage of being so small and nimble lets him move fluently between the tall, clumsy creatures like a fish navigating through a coral reef.

Soon he arrives at the Dockyard, but finding his father is more of a task than he thought; he glances around, panicked at the endless masses of people and uniformed soldiers as they filter through the market stands like animals at a cattle auction. Frozen and confused, the boy's confidence slowly deteriorates and emotion overrides the initial assurance, that is until a familiar hand reaches down to hold his and soon the unnerving anxiety is pushed aside by the loving embrace of his mother.

"He's up there Jack. Look!" She points to the back of a ship where a smartly dressed soldier is waving at the boy and his mother, "There's your father! Quick, it's moving. Let's get closer so we can see him better." Picking up the boy, she holds him tight and rushes to the front of a large congregation of other families saying their last goodbyes to the loved ones they may never see again.

The ship is pulling away from the docks when they finally get close enough and Jack calls out to his father, "Father! Father! I love you!"

"I'll be home soon Jack. Look after your mother for me. I love you Jack!" His father calls out to him. Then he shouts to Jack's mother, "I love you Abigail. I will miss you every day."

Abigail bursts into tears and is unable to say anything back to her husband, so she puts her hand on her chest, blows him a kiss and cuddles Jack even tighter than before as she feels her heart tear into a million pieces as the love of her life disappears into the distance.

Chapter 1

The Bastard Son

loud clashing of iron disrupts the early morning's peaceful melodic renditions. Through the dust being kicked up around the battle, a dueling pair strike and block one another's swords as they dance around a sandy courtyard, with each one taking their turn to deliver an array of stabs and slashes as the other parries the attack and prepares to strike back.

The young man is quick and well trained but being too determined to win the fight he loses focus and moves in too close, being met by the old man ducking out of the way of his opponent's blundering move and swiping away his feet with a swift kick. He pokes the sword against the young man's neck and roars with laughter. "You may be a man now Jack, but an old timer like me can still put you on your arse every time you challenge me! Get up and try again." He flicks his sword up and offers a hand to help Jack to his feet, "This time don't lose concentration. It's not about how hard you can hit, it's all about the timing and a well-placed attack."

The sparring continues and this time Jack watches and waits for the perfect moment to seize victory; as the old man lunges forward with a prompt jab, Jack pushes it aside with his sword, spins in and around the old man and finishes beside him with his blade on his throat.

"Looks like you're not the master swordsman anymore!" Jack mocks triumphantly.

"Take a look below." The old man grins as Jack looks down to find a dagger next to his crotch.

"You cheating bastard Nathaniel!" Jack exclaims, "You'd have been dead in a real fight long before getting that out."

"I might have been, however, you would have no balls afterwards!" Nathaniel bursts into laughter again. "Good move though. Let's go get a drink before I collapse from thirst."

"I've got to go to work. Our training went on longer than I thought. I'll be back tomorrow morning to see you though." Jack says as he puts his arms around Nathaniel and hugs him goodbye. "You know where I am if you need me old man."

"Thank you Jack. It was some great training today. Too good I need to go have a rest." Jack releases him and he retreats back to his workshop. "See you tomorrow."

Around the Dockyard, the markets begin setting up shop for the eventful day ahead; freshly caught fish hauled in and barrowed by the dozens to the local fish merchants who are keenly awaiting to put the colourful, inviting specimens on display. The haberdashers' stand selling all kinds of weird and wonderful items of clothing and materials, promoting the more mysterious objects that they claim were found in the deep, dark corners of the world to cajole the more elegant individuals in town. The local retired ship carpenter with his very own hand crafted wooden leg as a reminder of the bloody wars gone past of which he barely survived, now builds and sells his own furniture and offers his services for general repairs with a calm smile on his face but a distant and hollow gaze as a life of combat has left behind a shell of a man.

But behind the thriving marvels of the marketplace lie the more menacing citizens the town has to offer; the pickpocketing street urchins choosing their targets carefully and planning their daring escape if exposed. Then there are the brutish gang members ready to demand heavy tariffs from the merchants and traders or track down the poor beggars who have unpaid debts to their greedy, leeching bosses.

All are kept under a watchful eye of the naval guards, who seem more interested in trying to seduce the local women and accepting bribes from the generous criminals to turn a blind eye to the blatant misdeeds committed in front of them, lining their pockets with illegal riches and profiting from the strenuous sentry duties and the underpaying military wages they are encumbered with. Some would say the law in this town is more corrupt than the crooks that cower in the shadowy alleyways.

Jack finally reaches the shop and enters to a warm welcoming from his eccentric, cantankerous superior, "Well, don't just stand there and stare at me! Get out the back and sort out the list of uniforms that need sending out today!"
"Sorry Antonio, did you want me to pick anything up from the market today?" Jack asks trying to lighten the mood.
"No, I don't want anything from the bloody market! Sort out the list!!" He mutters to himself in Italian as he impatiently paces around the shop floor, "It's easier to do everything myself! I should just throw you on the street and you can go find another tailor to send to an early grave."
Jack ignores the mad rambles and disappears into the back store. It is filled ceiling high

with shelves of stacked clothing crammed into sections of the poor, the wealthy and the bits in between. The room appears to go on forever like looking into an infinite mirror; at one end of the store is a huge workbench surrounded by a variety of tools, spools of vibrant thread and an endless supply of tailoring equipment for Antonio to repair and create his masterpieces. The other end is where Jack finds the list of clothes and garments that need wrapping and tying, then to be delivered back to their owners. The shop itself is small and confined but well decorated and fashioned like a Roman Palace, with exuberant displays of lavish conceptions that would draw the attention of King George himself. Behind the cynical, petulant posture that years of wearisome labour has created and being cast as the runt of the litter in a foreign society, Antonio has a concealed charm as if cracking open a rock to find a diamond hiding underneath the stony outer layer, only presented when trying to sell his genius handiworks.

As hours go by of working through the list and continuous interruptions and complaints from Antonio, Jack ties the last knot and places the final package of the day onto the mountainous pile of deliveries ready to begin their journey back home to the dark and dusty wardrobes where they came from. Antonio appears in the doorway, but rather than barking orders at Jack, he seems more relaxed and empathetic now the day is nearly over, "Jack, I have errands to run and then I am going home. I just need you to polish the boots and fix a hole in the trousers that I have left on the counter and then you can lock up and go home. Busy day today, your work has got me out of a lot of shit. Tomorrow will be easy." He picks up his coat and makes his way to the front door.

"See you tomorrow Antonio. Have a nice evening!" Jack calls out as Antonio leaves the shop but receives no reply.

The trouser repair takes hardly any time at all, so Jack decides to take the boots outside to polish as the sun begins to set and the moon slowly creeps out from behind the horizon, ready to take its reign over the night sky and join the dazzling performance of the glimmering stars as they sparkle majestically over the darkness below.

Jack ponders and schemes as he brings life back into the tattered, timeworn boots. Like most days, he dreams of leaving his home behind and voyage over the high seas to find his long-lost father; most believe he is dead like all the other poor warriors that set sail for a greater cause but never returned. Jack is not one of them. He feels a calling. A bond too strong that will not be broken. A forever burning question that will never be answered. There is hope in his heart that guides him down a path of intuitive disbelief and assured faith that the stories played out in his surreal philosophies come true.
Yet, despite all the time spent with his head in the clouds, the boots are finished to a fine, gleaming perfection. He packs everything away and locks up the shop before making his way back home and narrowly avoiding the perilous gauntlet as

the streets fall to the gloomy terrors of night.

However, a commotion has stirred outside his house as a half dressed, drunken soldier has hold of a girl trying to get back inside. She pleads with him, "I told you I am not working tonight Joe!! Please leave and come back another time when you're not so drunk."

The soldier becomes more aggressive and forces her against the wall, "You're a fucking whore. You don't get to choose when you can and can't see me. If I want you, I'm going to have you whenever I want and if you're not working, then I guess it's for free."

She tries to push him off of her and cries out "Get─ off me Joe!! I'm warning─" but the soldier covers her mouth.

"Shhhhhh, you're going to shut up and enjoy yourself." He reaches down to lift her dress but is caught unaware as Jack throws a debilitating punch to his face just as he turns to see who is there, which sends him crashing to the ground.

"Get inside Andrea. He won't bother you anymore." Jack demands heroically as the soldier stumbles to his feet drenched in blood as he cradles a broken nose. "You come here again and it'll be my sword through your throat!"

Retreating, the soldier shouts out from a safe enough distance for Jack to not be able to engage him again, "Mark my words boy, I will have my revenge." Spitting away the blood that is pouring over his mouth, "Watch your fucking back."

Jack laughs off the soldier's threat and goes to comfort the girl inside who is waiting by the door with a knife in hand. "You know you really need to find another way of making money Andrea. I know you made a promise to my mother that you would look after me no matter what, but I don't want you dying too. Everything will work out well for us, I'm working on it every day. Soon you will have a life that you've always dreamed about."

Andrea drops the knife and hugs Jack firmly, "Oh Jack, you sound a lot like your father. Your mother would always tell me stories about him every day until she passed. They shouldn't have sent him on that mission. They didn't even do anything for your mother when he didn't return. She did everything she could for us. I know she wasn't my mother but to take me in as an orphan and raise me as part of the family—" She can no longer hold back her tears and cries into Jack's shoulder.

"You'll always be my family Andrea! You did everything you could. I'm here because of you. I know things are hard right now but we will get through this. Now let's get you to bed. A good night's sleep will make you feel a lot better tomorrow." He puts his arm around her and walks her to her bed, putting the blanket over her as she rolls over and closes her eyes. He gets up to leave but Andrea reaches over and holds his hand.

"Sleep here tonight." She asks softly.

"Of course. I'll keep you safe." He replies as he lies down next to her. "Goodnight Andrea."

"Goodnight Jack." Andrea mutters sweetly, letting go of his hand as she drifts off to sleep.

Jack takes off his jacket, kicks off his boots and stares out of the window from his pillow at the mesmerizingly starry sky and whispers to himself as he too can no longer keep his eyes open, "Don't worry father, I will see you soon."

Chapter 2

The

Unlikely

Soldier

orning comes by quickly and the restful nighttime peace is upstaged by the noisy surroundings arising like a clockwork ensemble. A ray of sunshine beams through the window and forces Jack to open his eyes. It takes a while for him to adjust to the dawning light but doesn't take him long to realise he may have overslept and should be stood in front of Antonio ready for his daily instructions. He throws on his clothes, stuffs his feet into his boots and ties his laces clumsily. Then, like Hermes delivering a message from Zeus, he races to the shop in the hope that Antonio is not in another one of his famous precipitous tempers.

Luckily for Jack, Antonio has been engrossed in an important order all morning and is oblivious as Jack staggers through the door panting like an over-walked dog.

"I'm here!!" He calls out to Antonio, readying himself for a wrath of fury, but instead Antonio calmly appears from the workshop with a large parcel.

"Ahh good! I need you to take this to Admiral Riley right away. I've been told he will be in his office at the fort. He knows you're coming so just tell the guards who you are and they'll take you up. He needs it right away so no dawdling." He drops the package into Jack's arms and goes back to his project.

Jack finds himself again hurrying nervously through the busy streets, clutching firmly to the parcel like walking through a lion's den with a gazelle carcass.

As he reaches the gates to the fort, he is approached by a group of guards who are eager to find out what is in the parcel.

"What's in there?" One of them questions as he tries to take it from Jack but is met with resistance.

"Maybe it's our extra guard duty bonus!"
Another one japes.

The first guard still has hold of the parcel
and wants to press for more information,
"You know I can have you thrown in a
cell for disobeying my authority. So hand it
over and I'll just take a look inside."

Jack still resists and decides to put the
egotistical guard in his place, "I'm sure if
you opened Admiral Riley's important
delivery from the tailors he would have you
stripped of your authority and put you in a
cell next to mine."

Letting go immediately, the guard backs off
and turns to one of the other soldiers, "You
can take him up. The rest of you follow
me." He swiftly cowers away with the rest
of the group to find somewhere to hide for
the rest of the day as one of them stays
behind to escort Jack to meet with the
Admiral.

The guard leads Jack through a maze of
corridors and stairs like Theseus hunting
down the Minotaur in the Labyrinth, except

Jack doesn't have a ball of thread to help him find his way back.

Eventually they reach a large wooden door defended by two heavily armed soldiers who instantly halt Jack and his escort.

"Who's this?" Demands the soldier blocking the doorway.

The guard nervously hesitates as he answers his superior, "Admiral Riley is expecting him. He has a special delivery from the tailors."

"Ok. Let me just check with him." The soldier knocks on the door and waits to be summoned.

"Come in." A muffled voice cries out from behind the fortified door.

The soldier enters and almost immediately re-emerges, gesturing for Jack to come through. Jack obeys and squeezes through the half open door and stands sheepishly in the middle of the room as the soldier shows himself out and shuts Jack inside.

Admiral Riley sits behind his desk like a King upon his throne; the desk itself could be used as a fortress and stands out as a prominent centerpiece amongst the other furnishings around the room. Huge banners hang from the ceiling and sitting between them is a piercing painting of King George, watching you judgingly as you move around the room and the burning fixation strikes fear in all who do not bow down to his hegemony.

On the other side, the Admiral has some of his glorious uniforms on display, with an endless amount of gleaming medals as a spectacle of his power.

Jack is caught gawping by the Admiral, who finishes his paperwork and sits back grinning, "Well, aren't you going to bring me my package or are you planning to move in?"

"Sorry, here is your package sir." Jack stutters as he hands over the prized possession. "I'll be on my way now."

The Admiral stops Jack before he turns to leave, "Don't go just yet." He points over to where his uniforms are, "If you'd like to earn a little bit extra, my boots need polishing."

"Of course sir," Jack agrees politely, "Would you like me to have a look at your uniforms too and give the medals a bit of a buffering up?"

"Thank you—" The Admiral pauses and waits for Jack to tell him his name.

"Jack Brook, sir." Jack answers.

"Admiral Jared Riley. You're not one of my soldiers so you don't have to shout out sir every minute. You can call me Jared if you want when you're in here." He says kindly as he gets back behind his desk.

"If you don't mind me saying, you're not what I expected Jared." Jack blurts out but instantly worries he went too far and looks down as he scrubs polish on the boots.

Admiral Riley starts laughing, "You thought I was an old, miserable prick who sits in his high tower barking orders all day long. Well, the second part is true." He leans back in his chair and shares a truth of his own, "I like you Jack. I used to know a few guys like you back in the war and to be honest, they're the ones who kept me alive and sacrificed themselves so that I could be here today. I was the only survivor of a viscous battle and barely made it back myself. We were all young and nobody believed we had the balls to fight, but those guys who weren't far off your age at the time fought to the very last man. One of them dragged me to cover and took bullets for me until we shook the attackers whilst many of the others left us behind and abandoned ship. He died on top of me and then I had to steer the sinking mess back here myself. Since then I can tell who I can and can't trust. I can see something in you Jack that tells me you have a good soul."

"I'm sorry to hear what you went through Jared. You are a hero yourself and I am sure those other guys were just as inspired by you as you were of them. And thank you for the kind words. I have lost a lot in my life too so I learn to appreciate things more and see things differently to others." Jack answers solemnly but tries to lighten the mood a little, "I better finish your boots though or you'll be barking your orders with polish all up your trouser leg!" The Admiral smirks and shuffles his papers, "I best get on with my paperwork too. I nearly thought I wouldn't have to pay you for not finishing my boots."

"Do you want to swap?" Jack asks cheekily.

"Oh, believe me, I would love to, but I have the honour of administering orders for a captain and his men to set sail tomorrow on an important mission that I've been assigned to carry out from those above me. So, lots of signing papers and sending letters and orders off to the men consigned with the task for me." He reads one of the documents closely. "The trouble is, I've got some of them injured or sick and not enough men here to replace all of them."

Just as the Admiral touches pen to paper, there is a knock on the door and a captain bursts into the room looking like he has seen a ghost, saluting and standing to attention maladroitly as he desperately tries to catch his breath. "Sir, I'm sorry to barge in on you like this— We have a serious problem with some of the supplies for tomorrow. I need you to come have a look and find a solution sir."

Admiral Riley rubs his forehead in frustration, gets up out of his chair, collects his things and turns to Jack, "Was great to meet you Jack. Hopefully we will run into one another again soon. When you're done, just leave the boots down there and I've put some money on my desk for you. Duty calls!"

"Goodbye sir. And likewise, hopefully see you soon and good luck!" Jack replies with a grin on his face after making a private joke with the Admiral.

The captain scurries off in front as the Admiral follows him begrudgingly and slams the door shut as they leave, confining Jack inside the office alone with his thoughts.

A perfect opportunity is exactly what is playing on Jack's mind.. This is his chance to carry out his own secret mission to help him on his way to find his father. With no hope in buying his own ship, and stealing one would be completely out of the question as it would be suicide. Even if somehow he survived, he would more than likely be left sailing it by himself without a crew and with the amount of holes left in it by trying to dodge bullets as he left the port it would not be long until it would start to sink.

He forges a new plan after remembering what the Admiral said about the injured and sick soldiers that he was unable to replace. Then sneaking up to the desk, he carefully searches through documentation, making sure each and every object that is moved goes back exactly how it was left until he locates the list of incapacitated soldiers and writes down their names on a piece of scrap paper.

He also notices the undisclosed assignment brief for which he may be a part of if he actually goes ahead with his daring scheme, but is taken back by what it involves. The document reads;

Search and Rescue of the ships 'The King's Voyager' and 'Pathfinder' that have been reported as missing in the last week. Their last known location was just North of the Flores Island in the Azores heading East to return home. Scout the area but do not engage any unknown ships. Reported sightings of Pirates South West of last known location. Thought to be involved in missing ships.

Heavy footsteps and loud voices startle Jack
as they gradually approach the door whilst
he is still noting down the intelligence he
needs to help him map out his next move.
Worrying he will be caught in the act, he
stuffs the paper into his pocket and makes it
look like he has just finished shining the
boots as one of the guards enters to check
on him.

"I am done now. Could you show me out
please?" Jack requests before the guard has
a chance to speak.

"Ok. Follow me." The guard answers
acceptingly and holds the door open for
Jack to leave the Admiral's office.

After twisting and twining through the
maze again, they finally reach daylight and
Jack shields his eyes as he adjusts from the
dark tunnels of the fort. He checks his
pockets to make sure he still has his notes
but realises when he can't feel any coins
that he left the extra money behind that the
Admiral put on the table for him. He

contemplates going back up but has already been away from the shop for longer than he expected and must get back to Antonio before he finds his stuff outside in a pile and a sign pinned up outside for a job vacancy. He decides to forget the money and makes his way back to the shop where Antonio is sat outside smoking. When he notices Jack returning to the shop, he throws him a set of keys and barks a sardonic comment at him, "I hope you haven't been fucking around all day!"

"No, the Admiral wanted help with his uniforms and boots. I told him it was a free service to keep him coming back." Jack retorts cunningly.

"Good. You're not as useless as I thought." He finishes smoking his pipe and picks up a bag sat by his feet, "I am going home so you can give the place a tidy and lock up. See you Monday Jack."

"Bye Antonio. See you Monday." Jack replies, excited to have nobody looking over his shoulder as he carries out the next stage of his master plan.

He locks the front door behind him and takes out the bit of paper with the list of names on it so he can search the store for a spare uniform that fits him. He is glad he kept the store neat and tidy as it does not take him long to locate and try on all the uniforms from the named soldiers he marked down until one of them fits perfectly. He wraps up the chosen outfit and boots in his jacket, locks up the back door as he leaves and rushes to find a familiar place to hide out at for the rest of the day and stash his stolen possessions...

"Jack!! Come and try out some of these new swords I've finished today!" Nathaniel calls out enthusiastically and darts out to give Jack a hug and take him inside. Jack does not seem as keen and wants to discuss an urgent matter. "Nathaniel, there is something I really need to talk to you about. Can we sit and talk somewhere?" Nathaniel notices the slight distress in Jack's voice and is quick to pull up a couple of chairs and pour them both a drink, "I did think something was up. Especially with whatever you're hiding under there." He points to the bulging jacket that Jack is cradling.

"This is very difficult for me to explain Nathaniel⸱⸱" Jack hesitates.

"It's fine Jack, you know I'm here for you and will do anything to help if you're in trouble." Nathaniel states understandingly.

"It's just hard because you're like a father to me⸱⸱ But it is something to do with my real father and I've been planning it for some time. Everything just lined up today and I now must do what I have to do. I can't stay here wishing and hoping for something I will never know the answer too. It'll eat away at me inside for my whole life if I don't try to find out what happened to him." He removes the jacket and shows Nathaniel the soldier's naval uniform, "I am going to board a ship tomorrow on a mission to find lost military vessels and hopefully I will find a lead of where to go next. You know how much you mean to me. I don't want you to be upset or mad with me."

"I'm not Jack, not at all. To be honest with you, I knew this would happen one day. You never knew what happened to him and I know in your heart you won't be able to let that go until you do. There is something very important I must tell you though which may change everything you are about to do and where your journey may take you?" Nathaniel insists.

"What is it?" Jack replies inquisitively.

"The man you are going to follow the path of is not your real father." Nathaniel confesses but holds his hand up to halt any questions as Jack's expression drops. "This is going to be lot to take in. Your mother never used to live like this; she came from a very wealthy family who moved from here to Jamaica so that her father could run a plantation and sell slaves. Her mother died young too so it was just her and her father out there. The trouble was, he was an extremely highly respected man throughout that industry and so he followed everything by the book and kept his nose clean so that he could wine and dine with the finest folk that invited him to their table. I have no idea who he is though because your mother never told anybody his name after what happened—"

"What happened?" Jack interrupts brashly. Nathaniel puts his hand up again and continues, "Your mother fell for another plantation owner's son and they became very close. Soon after, she fell pregnant with you out of wedlock and when her father found out, rather than helping her, he wanted to protect his name for the church and so not only did he disown her, but also sent her back to England with a threat to never tarnish his reputation. The poor boy she fell for had no idea what happened to her or was probably fed lies to keep him from pursuing." He pauses to catch his breath before carrying on, "And so she ended up back here, met your stepfather, Jonathan Brook, who although was not a wealthy man in the slightest, swore to protect and provide for you and your mother after they secretly wed before you were born. He was a good man and tried his best to keep food on the table and a roof over your heads until the day he joined the war. He left on a ship called Queen's Voyager."

Utterly lost as an unexpected knife of truthful oddity stabs deep into his heart, Jack calms himself through the aching despair and pushes for more answers, "Who is my father Nathaniel?"

"All I know is your mother kept a letter from him with the initials E.T. at the end of it. I'm so sorry Jack, I made a promise to your mother because it was the right thing to do for both hers and Jonathan's sake." Nathaniel bows his head in guilt of betraying his friends.

Jack immediately hugs Nathaniel, "You did the right thing for them so don't feel bad for telling me now. I will just have to find both of them. I am not changing anything; they both have something to do with my life and without knowing where Jonathan is and who E.T. is I can't carry on living this life here. Do you know if that letter is still here?"

"Yes, your mother kept it in the bottom of her necklace box. I know you have to go now and must do what you have to do

Jack, but just be careful and hopefully all I have taught you will help you find them. It has been a crazy evening so how about I hold on to your things so you can go home, sort stuff out and get some sleep, then come see me first thing in the morning as I want you to have something before you leave." Nathaniel says trying to not let emotions take over.

Jack grabs hold of Nathaniel and embraces him tightly, "I will come back Nathaniel. Like I said, you're like the father I never had and you will always be in my heart wherever I am. I just need to do this and then I'll come home. I'll see you tomorrow morning old man."

Chapter 3

Wrong Side
Of
The Law

ack spends the night in and out of sleep as his nerves turn his slumber into a nightmarish tribulation of anxious, sweaty awakenings until he finally gives up and finishes preparing everything for his leave.

Then it crosses his mind that it won't be long until he has to sit down and explain to Andrea.

He sets everything out ready and decides to wake Andrea to tell her so he does not miss his ride out of town.

Sitting down on the bed beside her, he gently strokes her hair and whispers to her, "Andrea, I need to tell you something."

She stirs and opens her eyes slowly, "What is it Jack?"

"There's a ship leaving today and—" He tries to explain but Andrea interrupts.

"No, I heard some of the sailors saying it's not leaving until tomorrow now." She mumbles still half asleep.

"Shit!" Jack curses and races out of the room to the front door, puts on his boots and hurries to the port to find out what is going on.

Bundling down the streets in blurred stressfulness causes him to lose his balance and crash into a couple of fishermen, knocking one of them to the ground in the process.

"I'm sorry." Jack immediately offers to help the man to his feet but he refuses and gets up ready for a fight.

"Watch yourself you little shit!" The fisherman threatens.

His friend looks closely at Jack and his countenance differs, "Wait a minute, you're the dead whore's boy aren't you?"

Jack sees red and lunges himself at the sniggering fishermen, hitting one of them in the throat and sending him backwards. The other one dodges the attack and throws a punch himself that catches Jack on the side of the face, but before he has a chance to retaliate they are swamped by a group of soldiers with weapons raised at the ready.

"Any of you move and it'll be your last." One soldier cries out as more scuttle their way through their comrades to make the arrests.

The three men put their hands up high and are chained together and dragged to the dungeons below the fort.

Luckily for Jack, as they are paraded through the market he is recognised by a girl who sidles through the crowd for a closer look. When she sees it is the young man she knows, she dashes off into the alleyways like a deer hearing a twig snap in the woods. She soon arrives at Andrea's door and bursts in without knocking, finding Andrea in the kitchen armed with a large blade again, ready to fight away any unwanted guests, but soon puts the weapon down when she sees who it is.

"Andrea, they have Jack!!" The disconcerted girl cries out.

"Who has him?" Andrea asks sternly.
"The soldiers have arrested him and were taking him to the fort! We need to help him!" The girl answers frenziedly.
Andrea grabs the girl by the shoulders and tries to calm her down. "Alice. Stay here and wait for me to come back. It's going to be fine." She sits Alice down and leaves to hunt down the man in charge.

Arriving at the gates of the fort, she approaches a lonesome guard as his colleague leaves his post for a toilet break.
"Excuse me, I am in need of your help." Andrea pleas with the guard.
Pretending to be nice to her through a sadistic grimace, the guard ripostes, "Of course I can help you, but it's going to cost you—" He reveals his vulgar intent as he takes Andrea's hand and places it on his crotch. "These shifts can get very lonely." Andrea smiles back at him, then suddenly intensifies her grip and squeezes his balls like the crushing tentacles of a mythical Kraken trying to smash a ship into pieces and pull it into the abyss. The guard

squeals in agony as Andrea makes her threat clear, "I need to speak to the man in charge here right away or I'll be feeding what's left down there to the stray dogs."

"Ok, ok. Just let go for God's sake!!" He beseeches with his eyes full of tears.

"If you try anything else I'll let your superiors know you were guarding this post alone and that you and your friend have been disobeying orders." She warns him.

"I won't! Please let go!!" He begs again and this time Andrea sets him free and waits for him to tell her where to go as he cradles his privates and unlocks the entrance for her. "Admiral Riley is who you need to see. Head up the main stairs, follow them around to the left, then turn right up another set of stairs, turn right again and follow the corridor down and you will see two men outside."

"Thank you." She says imperiously as she enters through the opened gate.

She eventually reaches the Admiral's Headquarters and only notices one guard on duty. He is distracted by a loud commotion down the corridor involving the second guard. Whilst he is readying himself to intervene, Andrea creeps up to the doorway, opens the door soundlessly and slips inside without anybody knowing, including the Admiral himself who is esteeming his new uniform and correcting his collection of medals pinned to his chest in the mirror. Andrea stands frozen in awe as she is drawn in by the Admiral's dashing demeanor and rugged handsomeness that she finds difficult to avert her attention from; with his delicate stubble sitting upon chiseled cheekbones and surrounding a neatly styled moustache and beard. A few scars on his face add to the masculine beauty and leave Andrea enthralled by the mysteries behind the man she sees in front of her. A moment of eternal perfection as if time itself had stood still and all the problems of past and present had disappeared and they were the only two people in the entire world together in just this one room. But nothing so unspoiled can last forever... The Admiral spins around and is given a fright by the silent girl stood in the entrance of his office, unsure whether it is

shock or embarrassment that has taken him
back,

"What on earth are you doing there? You
scared the life out of me!" The Admiral
gasps.

Andrea giggles to herself from the reaction
of the Admiral, "I'm really sorry. I came
to see you about something urgent and I
kind of got a little~ Distracted."

After seeing Andrea is no threat to him, he
laughs off the ordeal, "You nearly had me
ruin my new uniform. As long as you're not
a deadly assassin sent here to kill me then I
am sure I can help." He composes himself
and points to a chair in front of his desk,
"Have a seat. Next time knocking would be
a good idea so I don't give such a terrible
first impression."

"Don't worry, the first impression was good
for me." Andrea cheekily grins as she sits
down opposite the Admiral as he too takes a
seat behind his desk.

"So, what brings you to see me, Miss~" He
quizzes her for her intentions and to find
out her name.

"Miss? Are you assuming that I am not married?" She puts the Admiral on the spot. "Wishful thinking maybe." The Admiral smiles, but double checks before flirting again, "Are you married?"

"No. You had it right the first time— Miss, Andrea Shaw. And before you start getting your hopes up, I am here to have you release my little brother who was arrested this morning. I have no idea why, he is not one to ever cross the law." She reasons with the Admiral.

"What's his name? I will check to see if I have had anything come through to me." He strews through his paperwork to try and find a report.

"Jack Brook is his name." She replies. The Admiral stops what he is doing and looks at Andrea in confusion. "I know Jack— The boy who works for the tailor. He's a good kid. So you're his sister?"

"Yes, that Jack. I'm not his blood sister but his mother adopted me and I helped raise him after she died." She answers sadly. "But he means everything to me and I will do whatever it takes to keep him safe."

"Family are very important, I understand that. I will sort out the paperwork immediately and have him released." He states.

"Good, otherwise I'll have to tell your men I caught you posing in front of the mirror." Andrea jokes audaciously. "Don't worry though, I do the same when I am trying on my dresses."

To Andrea's surprise, the Admiral takes the joke well, "If you think that was posing, maybe you should give me one of your dresses to model!"

"I think you'd look quite nice in one, although you would have to shave off your facial hair." She continues.

"I think I would rather like to keep that on my face! Maybe I will leave the dresses to you as you would look a lot more beautiful than me in them." He responds flirtingly, but becomes slightly more nervous when asking his next question, "Speaking of dresses, would you like to join me for dinner tonight?"

"Has a common, street girl like me made the great and powerful Admiral Riley nervous?" Andrea teases.

"Just shut up and answer me because you do make me nervous, and I'd rather like to know if this wonderful, beautiful girl in front me would like to see me again this evening?" He replies playfully.

"Of course I would. But only when my brother is safely back at home." She demands with a smile on her face.

"Don't worry, he can leave with you." He hands her a small coin purse. "He also forgot his payment for when he helped me with something last time I saw him. Also, about tonight, I want to get you a little present so don't worry about getting dressed up too much beforehand. I have somewhere very special we can go."

"I bet you say this to all the ladies that enter this room." She mocks him again.

"It's very rare that I get ladies coming here, but when they do it is not for romance and nobody else has captured my affection the way you have today. You're extremely captivating, Andrea Shaw, and I

63

want to get to know all about you." He responds charmingly.

"The feeling is mutual." She says beaming with adoration.

There is a bang on the door and the Admiral shouts out to his next guest.

"Come in!" Then he apologises to Andrea for the interruption, "Sorry. Hopefully it's not too important. I'm enjoying my current company too much."

An officer storms through the door, salutes the Admiral and presents him with a stack of papers, "Sir, one of our large trade ships and its escorts have all gone missing around where the last ones have been reported."

"Shit!! How the fuck can they just all disappear? I need you to go down to Captain Burgess in charge of the operation on The Seeker and tell him to get up here right away." The Admiral orders fastidiously.

"Yes sir, right away sir." The officer agrees and rushes out of the room.

The Admiral turns his attention to Andrea again, "Sorry about that Andrea, I hardly get a moment of peace here. I have to tend to this right away. If you take this signed form downstairs they will release Jack right away and then later on we can eat, drink and enjoy each other's company without any problems."

Andrea moves around the desk to the Admiral, places a note in front of him and kisses him on the cheek goodbye, "I understand. My brave, handsome Admiral to the rescue! I will be eagerly awaiting your arrival later. I put my address on that bit of paper for you."

"See you later my beautiful, common street girl." He smirks and watches Andrea leave the room.

The thick, heavy iron bars screech as they are dragged open and a besmirched Jack is pulled from his rat-infested cell and handed over to his liberator, Andrea. The reunited pair hug and without saying a word she leads him out of the prison and back out to society to live as a free man once again. Once outside, they walk back towards town and Jack has plenty to say to Andrea although he is confused as to why he was released without any hassle. "How did you get me out?" he questions her.

"Turns out we have a mutual friend; one that has taken a fancy to me and wants to wine and dine me this evening. You didn't mention that Admiral Riley is quite the charmer!" She boasts to Jack.

Jack laughs but tries to show his protective side, "He does seem like a very honest, genuine guy and I think you can trust him, but you know what to do if his interest in you isn't sincere?"

"I know." She giggles and makes a cutting gesture on herself where a man's private parts would be. They both burst out in hysterics and then Andrea suddenly remembers the coin purse that the Admiral gave her for Jack. "He gave me this before I came to get you—" She hands it over to him, "Said it was for the favour you did for him when you saw him last."

"Thanks Andrea." Jack says as he puts the money away. As they walk a bit further towards the port he decides to stop her and tell her the truth about everything. "I actually owe you an explanation for rushing out this morning and getting in all this mess in the first place, but you may not like what you hear so I just want you to hear me out first. "Ok?"

"Ok." She accepts hesitantly.

"There is something that has been eating away at me for years and it is something I must do and can't be talked out of. Plus, I have found out that Jonathan is my stepfather and that my real father could also be out there too." He points to the targeted ship sitting in the dock, "I am going to board that ship tomorrow as a soldier and begin my search to find them both. I know this all sounds ridiculous Andrea, but I know they are still alive, I can feel something telling me to find them." He holds her hand and looks into her disbelieving, saddened eyes. "I don't want you to worry about me. I will come back. Hopefully with Jonathan and my real father by my side."

"I don't know what to say. I had no idea Jonathan wasn't your actual father. But that doesn't matter. I've always known you would end up like him and I have had many conversations with Nathaniel in the past about this. Why do you think he has always been insistent on training you so hard and teaching you the ways of the world? Deep down I just hoped you wouldn't actually leave. I just don't want to lose you Jack." She explicates painfully. He tries his best to comfort her as she cries her tears of sorrowing grief, "You won't ever lose me Andrea. I promise I will come home. I've spent years preparing things so you and Nathaniel can live happily for a bit without worrying about money. You know he will be here for you and look after you." He attempts to cheer Andrea up, "You never know, maybe if you marry the Admiral you can live in that palace with him and get a spare room for Nathaniel!" Andrea wipes her eyes and settles her sadness. "I think I would have to draw Nathaniel a map of that place or he would be getting himself lost all the time." Jack chuckles at the thought of a confused Nathaniel wandering in circles around the corridors and getting more and more annoyed as he enters the same rooms again.

"Poor Nathaniel. I promised I would go see him this morning so I should get over there or he'll come looking for me too. I'll meet you back at home later though?"

"Yes. I will be at home getting ready for my gallant suitor to come sweep me off my feet." She jokes as she refers to her date with Admiral Riley.

"Tell him to bring me a bottle of his finest wine too!" Jack returns as he heads off to find Nathaniel.

"Make sure you keep out of trouble this time or it'll be me having to buy the Admiral a crate of fine wine for releasing you from prison again." She calls out jeeringly as Jack makes his way towards the center of town. Then she turns to observe the ships as they are primed and equipped for tomorrow's expedition; the men carry objects onto the vessel one by one like an army of ants, fetching materials for their Queen's nest as the rest of the colony workers stow away the supplies and add more reinforcement to their fortifications. She takes a moment to let everything sink in, then she puts the thought of Jack's fate

to the back of her mind as she knows there
is no way of keeping him from his internal
battle for the truth.

Chapter 4

A New Beginning

unset invades the daytime territory and compels the light to retreat. The huge force of darkness approaches to take control of the skies and rule the lands until its reign is handed back to the morning daylight like an interminable game of tug of war for everlasting power.

Before the day has ended, Jack reaches Nathaniel's workshop and finds him packing up his tools and clearing away all the unused mess made from another batch of impeccable, metallic creations. They glisten and shimmer a reflective dance of flickering flames in front of the forging fires as if sculpted on an anvil by Thor himself.

"Hey Nathaniel! I've never seen you so busy!" Jack shouts out comically so his friend can hear over the noisy furnace beside him.

Although Nathaniel does not hear what Jack said to him but acknowledges his presence and points to the table and chairs set up outside, "Have a seat Jack, I have a surprise for you!" He yells in excitement and shuffles around his workbench like a child wanting to show their parents a drawing they did at school. He limps bouncingly out to Jack like his war wounds have miraculously healed overnight, with something long wrapped in cloth and places it on the table in front of Jack, "Open it! I have been working on this for quite some time so I hope you like it."

Unravelling the carefully covered gift, he reveals a handcrafted sword with detail so striking and magnificent it would raise King Arthur from the dead in a jealous frenzy, putting Excalibur to shame. A handle bedecked with gold, with a dragonhead pommel and a grip wrapped in its tail as it expands out as a knuckle guard, the quillon is covered in skulls readily waiting to collect the souls of the damned that stand in the way of their chosen master. The blade crafted from the most premium mirror-like steel with its edges and point so sharp that it could slice through flesh and bone like a hot knife through butter. On the bottom are the letters '*J.B*' engraved so it can never be parted with its rightful wielder.

Even the scabbard is detailed to supreme precision with encrusted gold and royal red leather fit to house the astounding weapon.

"I can't accept this Nathaniel. This must have cost you so much to make—" Jack stutters, mind-blown from Nathaniel's surprise.

"I didn't just come away from the war with a shattered leg. Let's just say I did my share of piracy before it became a hangable offence and still have some of the materials stashed away, which is what I melted down and used to make the sword." Nathaniel explains as he pulls out another cloth covered item and hands it to Jack. "The sword isn't the only gift. I thought these might come in handy too."

"But Nathaniel—" Jack pleads.

He interrupts Jack, "In here is a dagger similar to the sword and my lucky medallion that I had with me in the war, that believe or not saved my life a couple of times." He puts his hand on Jack's shoulder and reminisces, "You saved my life once Jack. Everything would have been lost or stolen, but now you can have what was once mine and make more use of it than it just sitting in a drawer of bitter memories."

"I don't know what to say― Thank you Nathaniel." Jack jumps to his feet and embraces Nathaniel.

"There's no need to thank me. You have given me a gift far greater than anything I could have ever imagined. You have been like a son to me, and after losing my wife I had nothing until you stumbled in here and changed my life forever―"

A wooden beam creaks above as an unsoundly man pulls on a length of rope below as he steps up on a stool and places a noose around his neck. The cold, rough fibres around his throat scratch uncomfortably as he pulls the knot tighter. Looking down at a necklace engraved 'Nathaniel & Esther' he edges closer off the stool and grasps the jewelry into a closed fist as he prepares to kick away the last object keeping him from life and death. Suddenly, his workshop door swings open and a young boy enters hysterically with a handful of bread and scurries desperately into the darkness and cowers behind some barrels without noticing Nathaniel, who cursorily takes off the rope that was meant to send him to his wife, steps down from the stool and walks over to the opened door.

When in the light, he signals over to the boy with a finger on his lips to keep quiet, grabs a sword and sits in the entrance pretending to clean the weapon as two frenzied soldiers approach.

"Have you seen a boy in a black coat come past here?" One of the soldiers wheezes.

Nathaniel points over to a house across the street, "I heard a bit of commotion over in that direction a little while ago but apart from that, nothing. Sorry."

"Thank you, sir." The soldier replies before they disappear through the alleyway opposite.

Nathaniel gestures to the boy to come out and join him, "Come here boy. I'm guessing what you have there in your hand you didn't pay for?"

"I'm sorry. I was hungry. We don't have any money." The boy answers woefully.

"You have to be careful. If they catch you they'll take your hand off or you'll end up in chains with the other criminals." Nathaniel scolds truthfully. "I may have a few things you could do around here to earn yourself some coin. Why don't you go fetch that bottle on the side there and come sit with me and we can talk business."

"Ok." The boy agrees and joins Nathaniel with the bottle of alcohol.

"So what's your name boy?" Nathaniel asks.

*"Jack Brook." The boy replies, warming to
Nathaniel slightly.
"Well, it's nice to meet you, Jack Brook."
Nathaniel raises the bottle and takes a swig.
"So how about we both look out for each
other from now on?...*

Jack hugs Nathaniel tighter, "You changed
my life too Nathaniel. I wouldn't be here if
it wasn't for you. I do actually have
something for you too that I have left with
Andrea. I know you're not going to accept
it which is why I left it with her but I
have saved up a lot of money over the years
and now you and her have to look after one
another, so it is just a little something to
help out."

"I know there is no point arguing with you
as you've got it all mapped out. I will just
say thank you and goodbye." Nathaniel
chuckles and ruffles Jack's hair.

"Goodbye old man. I won't be gone too
long. And if you get bored without me then
I'm sure Antonio will need another errand
boy." Jack says mockingly.

"I think the three-legged dog down the street could deliver packages faster than me!" Nathaniel replies and the pair burst into laughter.

"Make sure Andrea doesn't give you too much grief either. From how it all sounds you may be giving her away at her wedding with the Admiral. But I'm sure you will get to hear all about it from her. I just want you to always remember one thing whilst I am gone, you will forever have a place in my heart. I love you Nathaniel and I'll see you soon." Jack says as he prepares to leave his mentor and make his way back home for another sad farewell with Andrea.

"At least I can invest in a new wedding outfit with your gift then. And I will. I love you too Jack. Now get out of here as I don't like goodbyes!" Nathaniel demands jokingly as he holds back his tears.

Jack follows his orders and makes haste to see Andrea before he sets sail early in the morning. However, he is soon caught in a nostalgic recollection of past memories of his life spent within this town up until now; the memories play like a multitude of frame

narratives with each main character cycling
turns in the spotlight to express their
individual discourse to the audience.

The streets he now sees filled with scum
and pollution were once a fun and
mysterious playground where his father
would chase him around, play games of hide
and seek with him and would lift him high
above his head which made him feel like a
giant governing over his lands. Or the times
spent with his Mother in the marketplace,
when he would ask a million questions about
all the enigmatic wonders before his eyes
and pull excitedly on her hand to get her to
guide his curious erudition in everything new
that he had not come across before.

As the reminiscences flick through the
years, the unforgiving sufferings plague his
mind and even though the happy thoughts of
the years spent with Andrea and Nathaniel
remain protuberant to the rest, it is still the
despair and hardship they all went through
that burns away slowly like an obstinate
ember of an extinguished fire, desperately
fighting to find a way to relight itself on

anything willing to fall upon its burning
hunger for untouched happiness.

His thoughts subside as he approaches home
and finds Admiral Riley standing nervously
outside with a handful of flowers and
something wrapped in finely presented
material tucked under his other arm. He is
dressed in an enchanting uniform with his
hair combed and neatly pomaded as if he
was about to attend a royal wedding.

Jack is quick to evade the Admiral
momentarily as he is also carrying some
extremely precious items that might get him
sent straight to the gallows if caught with
the stolen uniform, or raise some questions
walking around armed with a sword. So he
creeps around to the back of his house,
climbs up to his window, drops everything
inside gently and returns to meet the
Admiral.

As the Admiral plucks up the courage to
knock on the door, he spots Jack, rushes to
greet him and tries to steady his nerves,
"Jack!! I was actually hoping to bump into
you! How are you?"

"I am good thank you. Are you doing ok Jared?" Jack replies.

The Admiral can see Jack has already seen through his façade so gives up the act, "Jack, how is it that I could lead our forces into war tomorrow but I am struggling to knock on the door and speak to your sister tonight?"

They laugh at the thought of how useless they both are with women, but Jack attempts to lift the Admiral's confidence, "You look like the King himself tonight Jared! I think she is rather smitten with you already, but don't tell her I told you that."

"Really?" The Admiral asks elatedly.

"Yes. Just make sure you look after her though, she has a huge heart but has been through a lot." Jack implores.

"Of course I will Jack. She is not like any other girl I have ever met. I am known for having a hard exterior when it comes to emotions but meeting Andrea changed that somehow. Even though it all happened so fast, she has engraved herself like a hot iron to my heart. I am glad I have your blessing though." He admits with heartfelt honesty.

"You will always have my blessing Jared. Although after tonight you will have to get Nathaniel's blessing, which will be the hardest task of all." Jack puts his hand on the Admiral's shoulder and smirks.

"Nathaniel?" The Admiral enquires hesitantly.

"Don't worry, I am only messing with you. Nathaniel is like our father. He has a heart of gold though. He is the best blacksmith in these areas," Jack points down the road from where he came from earlier, "He lives a few hundred yards down there in an old barn."

"I am glad the Blacksmith has a heart of gold and not steel! I have actually heard stories of the famous Blacksmith but have not had the pleasure of meeting him in person yet. I hope you are just joking with me and I make a good impression." He replies.

"I'm sure you will. Just join him for a drink and compliment his work a lot and you'll be the best of friends in no time.

Now, let's go and see Andrea!" Jack insists as he opens the front door and calls out for his sister, "Andrea? I have a surprise for you!" He shows the Admiral inside and ushers him forward to the kitchen.

Just as they enter the room, Andrea appears from her bedroom in just a robe and stops suddenly in shock as she finds her surprise standing before her bearing gifts. She smiles and admonishes the Admiral playfully, "Close your eyes Jared! You're not supposed to see me like this until we are married." Admiral Riley chuckles, closes his eyes and offers her his presents, "Well, looks like I'll be hunting for the best ring in the country tomorrow morning. These are for you by the way; The one on the right is a little something I got you to wear tonight, so at least I have saved myself as a gentleman and asked you to put on more clothes for me rather than taking them off."

Andrea takes the gifts and kisses the Admiral on the cheek. "You can open your eyes now and make yourself at home whilst I make myself pretty for you."

"You always look pretty." He replies. "You don't look too bad yourself. I'm afraid you will have to wait to use my mirror to check your uniform though." She mocks the Admiral and giggles to herself as he shakes his head and laughs as he remembers the moment they first met. Jack decides to make himself scarce as Andrea is distracted and get everything together in preparation for tomorrow, so he says goodbye to the Admiral quietly, "I am going to have an early night but enjoy your evening and will see you soon. I've never seen her so happy before. Goodnight Jared." "I will make sure she always has a smile on her face. And thank you Jack. Goodnight and sleep well." He says caringly.

Jack rummages through his mother's possessions hidden away in a safe place under a floorboard and pulls out the necklace box Nathanial told him about. Inside, he finds the letter to his mother and studies the initials at the bottom of the page before tucking it into his jacket pocket.

Then, once again, Jack finds himself staring out at the stars after packing away his most prized possessions and hanging up his uniform ready for its part in the daring operation to come. The reality of it all hits him hard and the years of fictitious dreaming and planning are now about to unfold and his time has come to lead another story⋯ To start a new beginning.

Chapter 5

All Hands

On Deck

is uniform fits perfectly as he stands confidently amongst a muster of other military recruits forming a queue to board the departing ship, completely unrecognisable and blending into the surroundings like a chameleon hiding from a predator.

As the line shortens, Jack is filtered closer to the front where an exasperated officer fires questions hostilely as he checks the approaching soldier's paperwork.

Jack begins to worry as he thinks to himself that this is not the time to stumble on his story and can only pray that the officer believes him and lets him pass by.

"Next!" The lieutenant yells, acknowledging the soldier standing fretfully in front of Jack, who then marches forward and snaps to attention with his documents out in front of him ready for inspection. The lieutenant snatches the paper from the soldier's hand, scans it thoroughly and places it back into the soldier's possession.

"Welcome aboard. Report to the master-at-arms for duties." As the soldier scurries onto the ship, the lieutenant shouts for Jack to step forward. "Next!" So Jack mimics the last soldier's performance, although this time the lieutenant frowns with anger as he notices Jack's empty hands, "You'd better have a damn good excuse for standing in front of me without your documents ready soldier?"

"Sorry sir, I was only released by the doctor earlier and was given a direct order by Admiral Riley to report immediately to you." Jack feeds the officer his lies assuredly and waits as the lieutenant turns to seek an answer from the captain, who looks up and leaves his reporting station to sort out the issue at hand.

He eventually reaches the lieutenant and moans at him in frustration. "Can't you see

I am busy? What is the problem here lieutenant?"

Equally as irritated as the captain, the lieutenant also vents his annoyance, "Those bastards keep sending me the incorrect paperwork and now they have sent me somebody from the sick bay without any documentation."

"I'm getting fed up with having to deal with these silly problems too." The captain replies and then focuses his attention on Jack. "Come with me, I may have your details back here." Jack follows the captain to his desk that is set up at the back of the main deck, where he then digs through a mountain of paper until he pulls out what he is looking for. "What is your rank and name soldier?"

"Corporal James Ward, sir." Jack responds. The captain studies the document and then looks down at Jack's legs with an expression of utter confusion. "Are one of those wooden?"

"No sir, why?" Jack answers, slightly puzzled by the captain's question.

"Apparently you're only supposed to have one leg?" The captain quizzes Jack further. "No, my legs are fine sir. I had a fever but the guy next to me wasn't so lucky; he had both his legs amputated so they must have got it all a bit mixed up. Sorry to cause a problem sir." Jack apologises to the captain in hope he will give up pursuing. The captain throws the paperwork aside and sighs with frustration, "God damn imbeciles! Just go and find the master-at-arms and he will hand you your orders."

"Yes sir." Jack obeys and scampers away to find the master-at-arms before the captain changes his mind.

He wanders around the ship and watches the systematic enterprise of clockwork soldiers, grinding through their laborious assignments like a machine engine opening up as each part plays a vital role to force the next component into action until the entire element is firing on all cylinders. Each cog turning one another smoothly as the well-oiled procedure gets ready to propel full steam ahead.

Right in the middle of the stage like an orchestra conductor, the master-at-arms towers over the men beneath him as he roars commands at those not meeting the desired tempo or falling out of beat of the working rhythm. His mighty stature and fearsome appearance is enough to send shivers down the spines of any man or being that crosses his path; with his uniform barely fitting his muscles and stretching it to extreme durability. Tattoos cover most parts of skin on show and from his chest they continue up his neck and onto part of his head, which is completely shaved and showcases the many scars of battle that resemble a complex map that only he can find his way around. Despite the frightening features displayed from afar, Jack approaches the monster of war to find soft, blue eyes that like the sea, are filled with mysterious, alluring beauty. He wonders if there is more to this menacing giant than what meets the eye.

The master-at-arms catches Jack's stare and signals him over. "So, you're Corporal James Ward then? Because you don't look a thing like the guy with the same name I served with years ago. Must be a big coincidence that you've got the same name and the uniform having all the same patches and repair work on. Anything you'd like to tell me?"

Jack panics now that his plan has been foiled, "I'll be honest with you sir, my name is Jack Brook. I just wanted to serve and do my part but they weren't taking volunteers, so I thought I would take over Corporal Ward's place as he is no longer able to join the fight. Can we keep that between us?"

With a small grin on his face, the master-at-arms winks and shakes Jack's hand. "You've got balls soldier, I'll give you that. I never liked the guy anyway. He was a coward. I would rather have you fighting by my side if that is what you are here to do." He leans in closer and talks quietly, "We all have secrets Jack. Also, call me Tobias. You need anything, let me know." Letting go of Jack's hand and leaning back, Tobias speaks loudly so that no suspicion is raised, "Thank you Corporal

Ward, your orders are to maintain order and running of operations in the galley. I will catch up with you later when it's time to eat."

Waking up in the loving arms of the Admiral, Andrea's date is still fresh in her mind as she smiles uncontrollably and cuddles closer to Jared, who is still half dressed laying on top of the covers with a small blanket over his legs. She still does not believe how dreamlike the night before was as she rekindles the moment when the handsome gentleman beside her covered her eyes, carried her to the top of a hill where he had set up a secret dinner overlooking the town; complete with table, chairs, candles and an arrangement of exotic flowers for them both to dine romantically as they overlook the moon-sparkled ocean and watch the world pass by in front of them.

After food, a few glasses of wine and hours of conversation that ran into the early hours of the morning, came the most perfect moment of silent infatuation when the Admiral leant in, placed a tender hand on her cheek and kissed her passionately; a moment of pure loving desire that had her heart feeling like it was going to burst. A feeling she has never felt before. A feeling like finding somebody who will become her everything. Somebody that fate brought to her to change her life forever.

As Andrea maps out her future with Jared, a sudden dreaded thought flashes through her mind as she remembers where Jack is and what he is about to do. She gently moves Jared's arm from around her, to be met only with a slight stir, a grumble and then he drifts off back to his dreams. She keeps very still and waits briefly before slowly sliding out of bed, tiptoeing out of the room and up the stairs to see if Jack is still in his room.

When she opens his door, the room is completely empty, with just a few belongings left behind that he couldn't take

with him. But on the middle of the bed sits
a letter surrounded by a bunch of flowers
and a large coin purse. Andrea picks up the
letter and begins to read through watery
eyes;

To My Beautiful Sister Andrea,

I am sorry I left without saying goodbye. I
hope you have had a wonderful evening with
the Admiral. I did not want to ruin it
all with an emotional departure.
Also, if he finds out what I have done it
may tarnish any relationship between you
both as it would make it very awkward
between you and him after he has to have
me hanged.

Jared is a good man though and it won't be long until I will be returning for the grand wedding!
You will find a large amount of coin that I have saved up over the years for you and Nathaniel to live comfortably on for a little while.

See you soon and make sure you look after Nathaniel for me.

Love you always. Jack x

In the corner of the galley, Jack joins
Tobias to eat his food behind the shadowy
curtains of darkness as the pair watch out
over the rest of the crew and tell their tales
in privacy, away from eavesdropping snakes
in the grass.

Although, one soldier stops scoffing his face
and shows particular interest in Tobias and
Jack as he glares through the other feasting
soldiers to confirm his suspicions. He leans
across the table and shoves the man's head
opposite him out of the way as Jack leans
forward slightly and is partially revealed by
a nearby lantern.

The soldier slaps his comrade's hand out the
way of his face, "What the fuck Joe?
What are you doing?"

The familiar character recalls his previous
run-in with Jack and draws the attention of
the others on his table, "That guy sat with
the master-at-arms is not a soldier. I have
unfinished business with him, but the trouble
is he looks kind of cosy with his new
friend. I know you boys have been waiting

to take down the giant for some time now—" He takes a swig of his drink and moves in closer to deliver his plot, "I've heard they've been planning a mutiny. Think we better get involved and save Captain Burgess. What do you think boys?"

Sinister grins around the table corroborate their part in Joe's revenge proposal as one by one they nod their heads, ready themselves with weapons and sit impatiently eager for Joe's next orders.

"Finish your food, wait until they get really comfortable, then I need one of you to distract the beast as the rest of us slip in behind and stick the pig before he knows what's hit him. The other one is mine— You lot hold him down whilst I slit his throat and watch him bleed his life away."

On the other side of the room, Tobias and Jack begin to find they have more in common than they thought and the pair continue their surreptitious conversation.

"So why on Earth would you board this ship if you weren't ordered to?" Tobias questions.

Jack surveys the area around him quickly to make sure nobody has moved in for a closer listen before spilling the truth to Tobias, "I've come looking for my father. Well, actually my stepfather first, and then find out who my real father is. My stepfather left for war many years ago but never returned. I know it's crazy because many were lost at sea or killed but I have a feeling he is still out there and I want to find out what happened to him and maybe he might have an idea who my real father is."

Jack's tale hits a nerve with Tobias. "Shit, that's pretty complicated. I knew I liked you from the start! I vow from this day on to help you find him. You see, my father was executed in the war along with many others taken prisoner by a Spanish captain after they lost a battle to him. But unlike you, I got to finish my quest quite a few years back before the Treaty was signed; I had hunted him for months until I finally caught up with them, attacked them at night and had my revenge when they attempted to surrender." He reaches out his huge hand and waits for Jack to accept his friendship. "Brothers?"

Jack grasps Tobias's hand and welcomes his new friend. "Brothers."

Out of the corner of his eye, Jack notices a suspicious character edging closer behind Tobias as he pretends to blend in with the background. His eyes give away his intent as they constantly flicker from Tobias to behind Jack, which confirms Jack's distrusting feeling that there may be more assailants closing in.

The engineered assault fails as Joe's trusted henchmen break their scripted strategy after Jack spots one of them advancing. The shadowy thug panics, pulls out a knife and lunges forward to deliver a fatal incursion on his unaware target. But before he raises his weapon, Jack picks up a blade off the table and launches it swiftly past Tobias's head and sinks itself deep into the assassin's eye socket.

Tobias jumps into action and boots the table across the floor, connecting hard against Joe, who in a desperate frenzy, charges frantically out of position to try his luck pouncing on Jack from behind. The heavy table smashes into his legs and he cries out in pain as he is sent crumbling to the ground. He then crawls to safety, scrambles to his feet and disappears into the mob surrounding the brawl.

Another two of Joe's goons appear from the onlooking crowd with swords at the ready. They split up to draw Tobias away from Jack, and after circling around them, one of them thrashes daringly at Jack, who ducks and dives out of the way and manages to pick up a chair to defend himself as he is forced into a corner.

The other member of Joe's gang aims for Tobias and tries to slice his sword down on Tobias's head, but is disarmed by a wooden stool that Tobias swipes up from the floor and after smashing it into the attacker's face, he grabs hold of him.

Jack is parrying vicious blows from his opponent with his chair until after a carefully placed block, he causes the sword to get lodged in the wood and twists the weapon out of the enemy's hand. Throwing his shield and potential weapon away, he then delivers powerful strikes to the attacker's face, knocks him on the floor and clambers on top of him. Then reaching for the nearest weapon, which happens to be a metal mug, he bangs it hard against the man's skull continuously until his head splits open and his brains are scattered over the floor as the metal caves in the bone. Realising the man is more than dead, he stops, sits back to catch his breath and looks up to see Tobias crushing the neck of the other one and dropping him to the ground like a ragdoll.

As Jack gets to his feet and moves to Tobias's side, they are rushed by a group of armed soldiers led by Joe, ready to pull their triggers at any given command.

"Do not move or we will open fire!" One of the soldiers call out threateningly, "You are guilty of inciting mutiny and committing treason. You will both stand before the captain and await immediate execution." He waves his hand to signal them to move towards the stairs, "Up the stairs to the deck, move!!"

Chapter 6

Calm
Before The
Storm

ound and beaten, Tobias and Jack are thrown before their captain as he draws his sword to execute the restrained conspirators. "You were planning on taking me down and making this ship your own then? I didn't expect this to come from you Tobias. You'll get to watch your friend die quickly and then I can take my time with you." He grins as he places the sword against Tobias's neck and looks over at Jack who is glaring vengefully at Joe. "Look at me boy!" He shouts at Jack, but after no response he moves the tip of sword from Tobias to Jack's chin and moves his head to face him, "Any last words scum?" "The man who set this up is right over there." Jack sets his eyes onto Joe again

who is skulking amongst the bloodthirsty crew. "You kill us and the real traitor behind this charade will be the one who stabs you in the back."

The captain lowers his sword, steps back and postpones the execution as he cogitates over Jack's tale and follows his gaze to see who he is talking about. The words have begun to spin paranoia and the fervently acrimonious captain is suppressed with doubt and confusion, creating a discomforting silence that drives Joe to bundle out from his hiding place to poison the captain's decision once again.

"These bastards were part of a mutiny! Kill them!! I'll do it for you sir." Joe begs like a rabid dog foaming from the mouth as he waits irascibly to be released from his lead to devour the injured prey dumped helplessly before him.

"There you go, captain, the snake has revealed himself to try and silence us before you found him out." Jack states to Captain Burgess.

Just as the captain finds himself in a peculiar position and the hesitation begins to show weakness in front of his crew, a panicked voice yells loudly from the front of the forecastle deck and saves further discomfiture, "Ship!! There's a ship approaching fast! Starboard side! They have a black flag raised!!!"

"Fuck!!" The captain curses in utter disbelief and his priorities change to a more troubling threat, "I can't deal with this right now," He points his sword at Joe and barks orders at the disengaged soldiers, "Tie him to the mast with those two and they can wait until afterwards." As some of his men grab hold of Joe and begin to bind him with Tobias and Jack, he rushes over to the side of the ship where the rest of the crew have gathered in a startled mass and notices that the approaching vessel is tearing through the waves at high speed, with cannons prepped and cries of war so hungry for battle even the obstreperous sea itself cannot upstage. In urgent distress, he screams at the top of his lungs "Prepare for battle!!! Fire on my signal!!"

The pandemonium unravels as every man and boy on deck race to their posts like a

colony of meerkats caught off guard by a
pack of voracious jackals. Some crash into
one another whilst others clumsily collide
into interfering objects that slither into their
path. One falls victim to an abruptly
emptied bucket, which found the back of a
boot from a rattled soldier, and as the water
sloshes across the deck, it finds an
unsuspecting subject that becomes the first
casualty of war as he slips awkwardly with
rifle in hand and lands heavily on the hard
wood beneath him, rendering him completely
unconscious and favourably better off than
being awake for the moments that are about
to transpire.

As the vehement marauder approaches, the
captain raises his sword high in the air and
waits for the perfect timing to rain terror
upon his foes and gain the upper hand. But
giving away his position and unaware that
down the barrel of an extremely skillful
enemy sniper, a carefully placed bullet has
been released and by the time the marksman
has taken a short breath, his target is hit in
the side of the head.

The captain slumps to the ground as blood sprays uncontrollably from a smoking hole left in his skull which tarnishes the perfectly pressed uniforms of his grief-stricken officers standing next to him. They look down in horror and once one of them finishes vomiting, he picks up the captain's sword in a desperate bid to avenge his fallen commander and waves for the attack to go ahead. The crew see the sign to light their cannons and begin to deliver an obliterating payback to the murderous bandits.

Although, the assault was ordered far too early and the entire barrage of projectiles land miserably short of their goal as they smash meaninglessly into the sea, only to find a long and lonely journey to the bottom of the ocean having unfulfilled their duties.

With barely any time to reload the cannons, the only option left is to brace for the opponent's retaliation that comes almost immediately afterwards without any vacillation as they turn their ship to unleash hellish annihilation.

Jack and Tobias wriggle themselves to the other side of the mast for cover, whilst Joe is more concerned with breaking out of his restraint.

In the matter of seconds, the opposing firepower explodes in a rapid frenzy and the ship is torn to pieces like it is made out of paper.

As if caught by Medusa's eyes, some of the crew freeze solid and make themselves easy targets for eagle-eyed sharpshooters as others scatter like animals at a watering hole when the lions arrive.

Tobias eventually manages to rip himself free and reaches over to help Jack, but they are both dragged sharply into the battlefield as a cannonball passes through Joe's head and the mast between them, blasting both into a shattering mess of bone, brains and wooden splinters.

Luckily, Tobias fell to the floor with ears covered and face protected, whereas Jack felt the deafening blast from the direct hit behind him and everything in his world suddenly goes silent, apart from the overbearing ringing and heavily muffled background commotion. He stares blankly at his friend as he tries to speak to him, but soon Tobias can see he is not able to hear anything he is saying and grabs him by the arm, points to the side of the ship and jerks him forward as the pair attempt to make a daring escape over the railings and into the murky waters below.

Again, another plan is cut short when a stray bullet sinks itself into Tobias's leg and topples the giant to the ground, taking Jack with him in the process.

As the bombardment continues and the gunfire increases overhead, the pair crawl to safety behind a bundle of barrels. Jack strings together a makeshift bandage for Tobias's wound whilst a peppering of bullets patter against their surrounding shelter like a storm of hailstones.

With his hearing returning gradually, Jack unravels a plan of action, "Tobias, I need to get you out of here. I've got to go and get my belongings. I can't lose my sword."

"Jack, no! I promised I would always be by your side." Tobias replies in agony as he attempts to move.

"I'll be fine. I need you to get to a safe place or we will both die here. Tie this around your waist." Jack demands, passing Tobias an end of rope as he begins attaching the other end to some of the barrels. "I promise I'll be right behind you!"

"You'd better be! I'm not going to end up as shark food by myself!" Tobias jokes and winces as he climbs up onto the railing. "Stay low and fast Jack."

Jack pushes the barrels to the edge and looks at Tobias to give him a signal to throw them over, but Tobias appears reluctant at first and then he nods begrudgingly.

"Good luck brother. I'll see you down there." Jack says as he shoves the barrels overboard when Tobias releases his grip. He rushes to the side to see his friend vanish beneath a swallowing portal of engulfing waves and watches until Tobias emerges from the domineering depths and clings to one of the wooden buoyancy aids tied to his body.

He then makes his way to the stairs,
ducking and weaving to dodge the flitting
bullets aimed at him whilst running an
assault course of dead bodies and falling
debris. He almost throws himself down the
stairs to get into some sort of cover and
searches through the darkness with his hands
extended out in front of his face to find the
sleeping quarters.

Wading through bloodied water and
squeezing through collapsed foundations of
the unsteady ruins as they continue to take
more devastating blows like a weary boxer
taking punch after punch with his guard
down.

Jack soon finds his belongings with a bit of
help from the light seeping through the
assortment of holes left by the cannonballs.
Miraculously, they are still sat on his bed in
perfect condition, so he takes everything out
of the cloth protection they are wrapped in,
straps the sword and dagger to himself
tightly and hurries back to the main deck
to join Tobias overboard.

As he is about to return to the deck, there
is a small explosion next to his head as

another unfortunately positioned shot hits one of the oil lamps, sparking the burning liquid alight and spraying glass fragments directly into Jack's face. Fortuitously, he moved just enough for it to only damage his left side, but not quick enough to save his eye as the serrated shards shred his vision into total blindness on one side. He screams out in pain, collapses onto the floor and shakily struggles to clear the glass. But as he attempts to adjust to the loss of eyesight, he notices the fire from the lamp working its way across the floor in the direction of some large gunpowder sacks.

In a terrified daze, he lumbers to his feet, dashes to the side of the ship and without any thought, dives over the railing just in time as he is followed by a huge fireball eruption that catapults him like a puppet with no strings in an uncontrollable plummet into the waters below.

The freezing saltwater draws the oxygen from his lungs and penetrates his wounds. The stinging blindness makes it nearly impossible for Jack to distinguish which way is up and which way is down as he thrashes frenetically to find the surface before becoming fish food on the seabed.

Through a thick curtain of blood, Jack can just about make out the distant light of fire shimmering through the tainted waters and uses every bit of energy he has left in his body to swim himself back to life.

He breaks through the harsh waves, gasps for air and spins around to find something to hold onto before his muscles seize. There is nothing. Just a thick smoke rising up into the darkening sky from the aftermath of utter destruction, but no sight of the burning wreckage itself.

Jack's hope fades as the adrenaline begins to run dry and the excruciating pain and fatigue bear a huge burden on his attempt to keep afloat as he treads water despairingly.

His working eye becomes heavy and his movement sluggish, the fight left in him is seeping out and everything tells him to give up. Defeated thoughts cross his mind; *maybe it was all a waste of time? Would I really find my father? I didn't even get to find out what happened to him. I've failed. Time to die.*

Jack slips into an insentience slump and he drifts into the unforgiving void below‒

The world around him turns to darkness as he slowly sinks into a tranquil abstraction towards a watery grave.

Except it is not his time to go just yet as a hand reaches out and pulls him to existence once again. His guardian angel, Tobias, lifts his motionless body onto a makeshift raft of barrels and rope with moments to spare as a mass shiver of rapacious sharks have gathered to feast upon the unlucky corpses or the even unluckier survivors floating unknowingly into the jaws of the monsters beneath them.

Tobias tries to bring his friend back from the dead as they are carried further across the open ocean with no end in sight.

Drifting over a boundless eternity as the commanding waves determine their destination, sea birds circle above in a ravenous battle against one another to win the chance to be first to feast upon the ripe flesh of the newly deceased carcasses. Tobias and Jack lie limply in a famished comatose as they wait for a glimmer of hope for survival. Jack holds onto Nathaniel's necklace and studies the inscription *'Nathaniel & Esther'* and mutters to himself, "Not yet old man. I made you a promise."

After what seemed like days of bobbing around on top of a never-ending journey of surreal abstraction, Mother Nature finally decides to spare them both and forces their raft to land, jolting them awake as it is conveyed onto the sandy shores of a seemingly uninhabited island.

Just up from the quiet beach there is a thick, dense jungle that keeps all the secrets hidden inside from outsiders. However, it does not discourage Jack from finding somewhere safe for them both to hide out, patch up their wounds and recover some energy to explore. He rolls over to check on his friend, "Tobias? How's it going over there? Are you still alive enough to carry me to shore?"

Tobias laughs and opens his eyes slowly, "I'm alive. But that's all I can do right now. How bad does my leg look?"

Jack moves to take a look at Tobias's leg and pulls the bandage up, "The bullet passed straight through and looks like a pretty clean wound to be honest." He glances over at the tree line and devises a plan. "We need to get into cover and try to see if there is civilization on this island. Preferably people who don't want to kill us!"

"Agreed!" Tobias replies as he sits up and then notices Jack's face, "Holy shit Jack! What happened to you? Your eye?"

"Yeah, I won't be using that again any time soon. The pain has sort of gone for now, just stings a bit and feels like I just need to rub it or open my eyelid but I can't. The rest of my face is just cuts and burns I think, so I'll be fine after I adjust properly. We need to get out of here though and find somewhere to treat our wounds so nothing gets infected. Can you walk on your leg?"

Tobias lifts himself up and puts a little bit of weight on his leg but buckles in agony, "Fuck!! I can't go anywhere with this. You go on ahead, I'll just hold you up anyway."

"I'm not going anywhere without you Tobias. Let me try and make a splint from these barrels and something for you to walk with." Jack states as he finds the energy to stand, then stumbling over to one of the barrels he tears it apart, finds the strongest planks and ties two pieces of wood tightly onto Tobias's injured leg as he almost passes out from the pain. "Come on, let's get off this beach and see what we can find." He helps Tobias up and pulls his arm over his shoulders to support him, "Lean on me Tobias, I've got you."

Tobias remains silent as he blearily staggers across the heavy sand and enters the gloomy jungle with Jack, where the sun almost disappears but twinkles across the leaves above as they pass below, penetrating the occasional opening with its beams of light as small gusts of wind bend the branches softly into rhythmic fluctuation, turning the undergrowth into a glittering dance floor around their feet.

They walk gingerly through the overgrown trail for another couple of hundred meters until they come across a naturally formed pathway that looks more like a supply route made by inhabitants and not just more stranded castaways taking a guess at what direction to take.

Jack takes a moment to compose himself and gain some strength back after having to take most of Tobias's weight, who has been progressively diminishing since they entered the jungle. Jack knows that if they stop now they may not survive without food and drink and somewhere warm to recover. He looks at the tracks and decides to follow them to the right, where more of the shrubbery has been flattened down to face a particular direction and shifts Tobias down the course with him, "Tobias, we just have to keep going a little longer and then we can rest. Hang in there brother!"

As night creeps up behind them like an assassin shadowing their target, waiting for the perfect moment to pull the world around them into darkness, Jack is rattled from his sleepwalking trance by sounds of indistinct singing and shouting that he first thought were tricks playing on his mind. As they follow the noise they break through into a town as it is preparing for bed whilst the unsleeping laggards are partying and causing disorder further down by the seafront.

Jack shakes Tobias to announce his finding and to try and urge a boost of adrenaline for the last push to find somewhere to hide, "Tobias! Look! We're saved. Just need to find a safe place and somebody to help us."

"Where are we? I need to sleep Jack. Lay me down." Tobias mumbles.

"No. Not yet. I have no idea where we are, but it's almost nighttime so should keep us fairly covered. Let's go. There must be a barn or somewhere quiet around here to hide out in and then I'll go find some supplies." Jack answers and guides Tobias towards the houses in front of them.

They stagger through the buildings until Tobias gives up, bringing them both down to the ground with a loud thud as he collapses. Jack gets up and tries to help Tobias to his feet, "Get up Tobias, we are almost there. Don't give up on me now!"

"I can't walk anymore Jack." Tobias susurrates in exhaustion.

Before Jack can say another word, a door swings open from a nearby house and out steps a large, robust woman who has come to see what all the racket is, "Oi!! You two! What the hell are you doing?" She shouts out as she approaches, "Has your pisshead friend had a bit too much?" cackling to herself until she suddenly stops and whispers in horror when she gets closer, "You're soldiers? Do you have any fucking idea where you are right now? I'll hang you up myself!"

As she backs off, Jack lets go of Tobias and moves towards her with his hands up and explains who they are before they are cut down in the street, "Wait. It's not what you think. We aren't who you think we are."

"Don't come any closer. Tell me who you are then?" The lady demands.

"I am Jack Brook and this is my friend Tobias. I sneaked aboard a British Navy ship so I can find my stepfather and my real father. The Spanish Navy hanged Tobias's father years ago so he joined the British Navy to work his way up and get high enough to take revenge on the man that ordered it. After doing so, he is now helping me find mine. Our ship was destroyed and we washed up on the other side of the island. We just want somewhere to recover and then we can be on our way without any trouble."

The woman takes a moment to let Jack's tale sink in and looks further to see the state they are both in. "Wolves in sheep's skin eh? You'd best get him inside as fast as you can and I'll patch you two up. I'm Maggie by the way." She goes back into her house and leaves Jack to drag Tobias to her door. Once inside, Maggie gives her next orders to Jack as she rattles through her cupboards, "Clear the crap off the table and put him on there. Then I need you to fill that bucket over there with some water and fetch me a few rags from the other room in the basket by the fireplace."

"Ok." Jack replies, moving various items off the table and using all the strength he has left to lift his friend onto it. "Tobias, I need you to give me hand here because you weigh a ton!" Tobias tries to help and groans as he is moved around. Finally Jack manages to lay him down, then he gathers the towels, fills the bucket and returns to the kitchen. "Thank you for helping us Maggie."

"You can thank me later. First you can take a seat and relax whilst I take a look at his leg. Here, drink this." She hands him a bottle of rum and investigates Tobias's injury. "Your friend is very lucky, looks like the bullet passed straight through and no sign of major infection. I think he's just lost a lot of blood so will need some sleep and plenty of food and drink. I'll get some stronger alcohol for it, sew up the wound and then we can take a look at you. Can you see out of your eye at all?"

"No, nothing. I think whatever got in there cut it all up pretty bad but I'm sure all the glass must have come out when I hit the water. It's starting to hurt now though but can't feel if anything is still in there."

"At least you've still got the other one I guess. Might make aiming a rifle easier!" Maggie smirks as she tries to lighten Jack's mood.

"True, if I lost the right one I don't know how the hell I would hold a rifle in my left arm." Jack swigs the rum and decides to find out more about their saviour, "So what is it you do around here Maggie?"

She teases him with her answer, "You know if we become friends it doesn't mean you two get to stay longer!"

"Damn, I was just starting to like it here too." He joins in with the joke.

"You'll be begging to leave after the long list of jobs I will have for you once you're back in action." She laughs through the concentration as she pushes and pulls the needle and thread through Tobias's wound. "But going back to your question, I try to keep things in order here on this island; not too sure if you know exactly where you are but this is a safe haven for outlaws. Mostly pirates stay here to resupply, trade and spend some of their takings, but recently there are less and less of them coming here because of the numerous monarchs who want something to do after the war and so decided they would rather hunt the men they once used as privateers. The other sons of bitches joining them are the traitorous scum hired to hunt down their own kind for measly bounty rewards or a pardoning bargain. You will probably find some of those strung up by their necks down by the docks. Anyway, I run a brothel to help the boys shake off some of their testosterone as it can be rather lonely out at sea for weeks or months on end. But don't think for one minute that my girls are forced to do this; the guys pay well, they choose who they want and the men know my girls run this town so they rarely step out of line. Although, we are having problems with a new gang leader after the last one died. The previous leader and I had an agreement, but this scumbag is stirring up a small storm. Sorry, I went a little off topic there; I'm like a mad beggar sometimes with my ramblings. What I was thinking is that you two could work for me as I need some extra security around the place and to look after the girls. You will be paid well for your services and you can stay here and nobody will have any idea of who you were and where you came from. What do you think?"

"Shit, I didn't realise how bad it was for pirates out there. And of course we will help you! You could have just turned us in straight away but you didn't. You saved our lives. We are here to help until you don't need us anymore. Maybe whilst I am here I can see if anybody knew my stepfather or father." Jack replies optimistically.

"What are their surnames? I'm not too great with first names but sometimes it's a surname that sticks in my head." Maggie quizzes as she finishes stitching Tobias's leg.

"My stepfather— Brook. And his first name was Jonathan. My father— I don't know, but I'm hoping Jonathan does if he is still

out there." He answers in hope something
will jog her memory.
She pauses and deliberates before responding,
"It really rings a bell but can't put a
finger on why I know it. Sorry. My brain
is a bit foggy tonight." Her eyes light up
as an idea crosses her mind, "I tell you who
might know though⁓ There is a Pirate
King that goes by the name of Blackbeard.
He is in town with his crew for a few days
so I'm sure if you're up to it tomorrow
night you could try and ask him. Be careful
though, I've heard many tales about him
and his men that make your skin crawl.
Don't know how true it all is but just be
watchful around them."
"Thank you Maggie." He says
appreciatively.
She finishes the sewing and bandages Tobias
up before moving onto Jack, "Right, he's
done. Now it's your turn." She moves the
bucket of water over to where Jack is
sitting and pulls her chair in front of him
to get a closer look at his injuries. "I think
you already know there's nothing we can do
with that eye. My husband⁓ God bless his

soul– Lost his eye on the same side as you from a ricocheted bullet in the war, so I made him a very fetching leather patch you can have. All his stuff is sat upstairs collecting dust anyway."

"I'm sorry for your loss Maggie." Jack comforts as Maggie begins to clean his cuts with the water from the bucket.

"Thank you Jack. He was a war hero, but when he came back he couldn't do much after losing his arm and some of the sight in his good eye. He would drink himself silly and gambled away any riches he had left in life. In one way it paid off because he won the brothel in a stupid game they used to play, but the more he would drink, the more he upset people and eventually rubbed somebody the wrong way and he was beaten to death by a group of soldiers. The old gang leader, who I mentioned before, bearing in mind this was before he had properly set up an illegal operation here, well, he was good friends with my husband Carl, so he went after the soldiers with his men, killed them all and put them up on spikes. After that, he gave me half the town to run my business in and he took the other half for his. Ever since then this town has been an outlaw haven and over the years I have had my girls arrive from all different walks of life. They are my family now since Carl died. They are just as dangerous and feared as the Pirate Kings in these areas."

"I would have loved to have met Carl. I would be more than honoured to wear his patch too and to meet the rest of your family tomorrow night." Jack states deferentially.

"He would have liked you. I think the girls will too! I think these battle wounds add a more menacing, mysterious side to the young, handsome one." She sits back and nods in agreement with her own avowal and then gets up to go clean her hands. "The burns sealed the cuts pretty well so will just take time to heal and scar. I will go find Carl's patch and set up your beds for the night. Help yourself to food on the side. Make sure Tobias eats something and drinks plenty of water."

"Thanks Maggie." He says as she leaves the room. Then Jack moves over to his friend's side as he regains consciousness, "At least you know you're not in heaven seeing this face!" He jokes with Tobias, who smiles back at him.

"Fuck me Jack. What happened?" He blurts out and laughs as he tries to recall how they got from the raft to Maggie's house.

Jack laughs with Tobias and squeezes his friend's arm, "I'll tell you about it in the morning. It did involve having to carry your heavy arse miles through a jungle though. But first we need to get you to bed and then we can talk about how many drinks you owe me tomorrow."

Chapter 7

Welcome To The Family

fter a long rest, Jack surfaces from his bed like a bear emerging from hibernation and stretches his arms and back before groaning loudly as he tries to stand and force the reluctant, aching muscles in his legs to function properly.

Tobias is already awake and chuckles as he watches Jack struggling, "You look worse than me!"

"Fuck off Tobias!" Jack says frivolously as he rubs his legs where it feels uncomfortable, "Try carrying you halfway across an island. I'm surprised I can still walk." He looks up at Tobias and they laugh at each other.

"Fair point. At least it's all muscle and not fat." Tobias claims.

"That's worse! Plus, I'm carrying the extra weight of all the shrapnel you've collected in your body over the years." Jack pronounces.

"Very true. At least when I die I might be worth quite a bit when you burn my body and all you're left with is a big block of melted lead and steel." Tobias jokes and knocks on his head, "Mainly lead."

"Now that you're the better looking one of us, you'll be pleased to know Maggie wants us to meet her girls at the brothel tonight. We're the new security." Jack explains.

"It's already getting dark outside so we must be needed soon, although I think we should have a few more hours of rest. I'll go see if Maggie has anything that can help you walk with. Do you want anything else? Food? Drink?"

"Yeah, could you get me some water and a bit of food if there's any going. And I thought I was the better looking one anyway? Also, I was going to say, I don't think I am going to be the best security

trying to hop after somebody." Tobias
replies as he sits up in bed.

"Very true¬ I'll find you something to
throw at them instead! Right, I won't be
long." Jack says as he leaves the room.
When he reaches the kitchen he finds
Maggie pacing angrily back and forth and
wonders what has been going on to have
riled her up so much. "Everything ok
Maggie?"

She stops when she hears Jack's voice and
passes him a note that has been scrunched
up in her hand, "Sorry Jack, I've been
having some issues with the new gang
management lately and now I have received
this from somebody I know on the inside.
Read it and see what you think I should
do."

Jack unfolds the paper and takes a look;

The Dentist is planning to
try and muscle you out so
he can take over the whole
town. I don't know any
more than that I'm afraid.
I will try to find out
more but I have a horrible
feeling they already suspect
something and I think I
am being followed. I am
certain he had something to
do with our friend's death
and the disappearance of
Sharky Sam and his wife
after he was meant to take
over Leadership. This guy is
dangerous so just be careful
and I will try to help as

much as I can. We will
meet in the same place but
I will walk past if I
feel like I am being
tailed.

"So this '*Dentist*' guy is now running the
other part of town?" Jack asks after
handing the note back to Maggie.
"Yeah. He hasn't been part of the operation
for long; he arrived about five months ago
with around three or four other men with
him in a small boat covered in blood. They
claimed their ship was attacked and the rest
of the crew died so they needed a new place
to stay. We had heard tales of a man that
went by the name '*Dentist*' so we were
weary to begin with, but they seemed to
want to help and be part of the town.
After a while he fell into the ranks and
they kept to themselves until people starting
dying mysteriously or disappearing off the

face of the Earth. It all makes sense now though. Shit." Maggie exhales deeply and rubs her forehead.

"Why the name Dentist? And what were the tales?" Jack quizzes curiously.

"He pulls gold teeth from the dead he comes across and people he has killed personally, which is normally during or after his barbaric torture treatments. Then he rips out his own teeth to replace them with the gold ones. The tales vary; one is that he used to be a spy during the war for the Spanish, finding information on enemy whereabouts and cargo information, but then after the war they sent assassins to have him killed because he found out a bit too much and he thought he was more important than he was. I don't know, most people here have done some pretty awful things so we can't really pick and choose what outlaws are welcome or not." She explains to Jack.

"I guess you never know the real truth sometimes. Sounds like we do need to keep our guard up though as we can't just take it as a bluff." Jack warns after processing

143

everything being said. "Is it something we could ask Blackbeard to help with?" Maggie sits down and pours them both a drink. "Sadly, Blackbeard won't get involved in this sort of thing unless it affects him directly. I wish he could help us though." She comes up with an idea after sipping her drink, "You could still try tonight after he has had a few drinks and then you can take them over some more and catch his attention."

Jack looks off into the distance as he wonders how he could bargain with the King of Pirates. "I will have a think and hopefully I can sell him a good enough deal to get rid of the Dentist."

"Thanks Jack." Maggie gulps down the rest of her drink and gets up to leave with haste, "I forgot I have to get some bits in town for tonight but I'll be back later and we can head over to meet the girls if you two are feeling up for it?"

"Ok, sounds good to me. Let me know if you need a hand with anything." Jack states as he also stands to gather the bits to take up to Tobias.

"I'll be fine. Thank you though. See you later on." She replies and makes her way out of the house.

Jack returns to Tobias with what he asked for, but he is fast asleep so leaves it on the side for him and decides to get some more rest before the evening's escapades begin.

"Wakey wakey sleepy heads! Time to come meet the girls!" Calls Maggie as she enters the room carrying a bundle of clothes and a wooden crutch tucked under her arm, "I thought some of these might fit you guys. Tobias, I got a few things for you in town as I didn't think you'd fit all those muscles into my husband's old stuff. And I got you something to help you walk around a bit with." She separates the items and places them by their beds as the pair gather their thoughts after being abruptly awoken. "I also have something for you Jack." She reaches into her pocket and pulls out Carl's eye patch, which she holds to her heart for a moment before handing it over to Jack. Jack accepts the gift and tries it on. "Fits perfectly. Thank you Maggie."

She smiles through heartache and changes the subject, "When you are both dressed and ready, come downstairs and I'll re-patch your wounds and then we can get going. You guys still ok to come along?"

"Of course!" Jack replies.

"Yeah, although it might take me a little longer on the crutch. Jack said he would carry me again though." Tobias laughs as Jack raises his eyebrow, grins and shakes his head.

"I nearly died the last time carrying you. I'll tie you to a horse this time!" Jack teases him.

Maggie laughs in amusement and leaves Tobias and Jack to get ready, "Don't take all night. I'll see you in the kitchen shortly."

Jack stays close to Tobias as he hobbles uneasily through the town as they follow behind Maggie, who is continuously stopped and greeted by her friends and business associates. Eventually they reach the tavern without any trouble and Maggie directs them both to the entrance.

Once inside, they see why this is the most popular establishment in these parts; the décor resembling what one would assume the King's Royal Ship Quarters looks like, with a grand staircase leading to multiple rooms situated along a balcony that overlooks the bar below. The girls can survey the area like eagles soaring high above their prey, undetected as they select the most fitting game to feed their needs.

"Mother's home!! I have two new members of the family for you all to meet!" Maggie yells out as she retreats behind the bar. "Take a seat guys, I'll bring you over some drinks."

Jack pulls out some chairs and supports one as Tobias flops inelegantly onto it. As he sits down himself, he taps Tobias on the arm and points over to Maggie as she is lining up an arsenal of weaponry across the counter and one by one she examines them to check if they are loaded and then rehomes them to various accessible hiding places.

The evening's entertainment evolves progressively when the unforeseen mobocracy erupts in response to Maggie's words like beggars vying for scraps from a crashed food cart. The girl's doors fly open and they each appear on the balcony to get a look at their new toys. They giggle and whisper amongst themselves but soon they hush their colloquy and turn to wait instruction from their superior as she graces the staircase with fearsome elegance; her fiery red hair flowing flamingly with every descending step she takes, her muscular physique and bodacious curves bursting through her black armoured corset and filling her tight leather trousers.

Like moths to a flame, the other girls follow their beacon of light, each one possessing a unique display that fulfills their story and intrigues their audience; inimitable flowers ready to share their pollen with the wasps and hornets swarming in to find a new patch of nectarous trophies.

When the goddess of war reaches the bottom step, Jack springs to his feet and pulls Tobias up with him to formally greet the deities as they gather around the table and await an introduction.

Their doyenne speaks first, "I've never known this place to bring in such gentlemen." She glides around behind Jack and kisses him on the cheek before pushing his shoulders gently to sit him back down, "You look like you've been in the wars, so just relax and we'll show you a good time." Still holding onto Jack, she orders one of the girls over who hasn't taken her eyes off of Tobias since leaving her room upstairs, "Noose! I have never seen you look at a man in such a way. Give the poor guy some help getting back on his seat." The girl smiles shyly and then makes her way over to Tobias as her boss lets go of Jack and pulls a seat up to the table. "I am Phoenix. What are your names? And what brings you to our little paradise?"

"My name is Jack Brook and this is—" Jack replies and waits for his friend to respond, however Tobias is a little bit distracted as the girl sent to help him is now sat on his lap and reading his scars like she's translating a story in a lost language. "His name is Tobias. And the reason for us being here is that I am on a journey to find my stepfather, Jonathan Brook, and my real father who I only know by his initials from a letter. So far, as you can tell it hasn't been going too well for us. We kind of washed up here after our ship was blown to smithereens."

"Another hero's tale." The red-haired woman says with admiration. "I guess it's time to hear our stories now. Well, I used to live in a little village far away from here. I was very young when I fell pregnant and had a little girl from a man who was too devoted to his own family to care for a new one, so he left us to survive on our own. When my daughter was ten she began asking questions about her father so I decided to track him down and confront him. When he couldn't kill me himself to protect his heinous affair from his wife, he protested to his religious dogs that my daughter and I were witches and so we were captured, paraded through the streets and bound to a stake for all to watch us burn alive. The idiots didn't see a storm coming so the fire only burnt half of my body before the rain came down and put it out.

They thought it was our black magic that made the storm and that we were too powerful to destroy so ran away in fear to pray for us to leave town. I freed us from the ropes and thanked the heavens above for putting out the fire, but my daughter was not lucky enough to survive her injuries. I fell into the pits of Hell for a long time until I rose from the ashes to avenge my daughter, which is exactly what I did— I returned to the village to find them all praising their Lord for taking us away and then waited until they were all sleeping peacefully, then I set each and every building alight after blocking their exits and watched as they were all cooked to death in front of me. Any survivors that managed to climb through windows met the end of my blade. I made sure my face was the last thing they ever saw in this world. I carry our flame together through life until I can meet her again on the other side. Who I was before is dead, now I am Phoenix." Maggie puts a tray of drinks down on the table and passes one to Phoenix. "Thanks Maggie. Now for the rest of the girls—"

She knocks back her drink and gestures for
the first girl to present herself, "I'll let
them tell you themselves."
The first girl is dressed in an oriental dress,
with her black hair tied up to show her
angelic, flawless beauty that the seraphs
above would fight over in jealousy. She
takes a sip of her drink and begins her
story, "I am Pearl. The Chinese Princess.
Or Princess of Death as some know me by.
I was taken as a child and sold into
slavery, where I found myself in the hands
of some evil people; they would torture us
and use us any way they wanted to. One
night I took some knives from the kitchen
and as they were sleeping with their other
slaves, I killed them all one by one as they
lay in their beds. Then I freed all the
girls, shared out the riches left behind, then
covered my body in tattoos to hide the scars
they left me with and escaped the country
on the next ship leaving and found myself
here. Then I met Maggie and Phoenix."
The next girl to step forward is a blonde
divinity in the form of a Pirate Queen, with
two loaded flintlocks and a shiny cutlass

strapped to her body. They cling to her
blood red corset, fitted perfectly to the
colour of death that they are soon to create.
A selection of interesting collective trinkets
dangle from her waist and each object
appears to show significance to the girl's life
as they sit comfortably amongst the fabric
of her skirt. She picks up a nearby chair
and takes a seat next to Jack. "I found my
way over here from Ireland. I was bored of
that life and had enough of being poor and
slaving for pittance, so I decided to leave
with a friend I knew from home and had to
disguise myself as a boy until I reached
Nassau. My friend became really ill and
died on the journey so I arrived with
nothing and nobody by my side. That was
when I met a new friend, Mary Read. She
was good fun and we became close friends
quickly. We would always go out dressed as
men to rip off merchants and make a bit of
money. Then she disappeared for a while so
I decided it was time to move on and go it
alone, which didn't go too well. After
getting myself into a lot of trouble and
managing to evade punishment, I ended up

making money and keeping myself well protected by spending my time with powerful pirate captains. That's where most of these came from." She shows Jack some of her jewels before continuing, "One of these is from the great Benjamin Hornigold! Some of them are memories of my past and some I prised from the clutches of dead men who tried to own me. I guess I am still waiting for my true love. That's why they call me Aphrodite."

The last girl to answer is still attached to Tobias as they listen to the other girls. She looks over at Phoenix and holds her hand over a choker she is wearing around her neck. Phoenix nods her head and begins the story for her friend, "Last but not least, is Noose. She was married to a Spanish privateer, turned pirate. She joined him on one of his operations but ended up outnumbered and outgunned so they had no other choice but to surrender. She was to be hanged first in front of her husband, who managed to break free from his captors, grab a sword from one of them, cut her loose before she suffocated to death and then

after taking multiple bullets he still managed
to get them overboard to safety. He was
shot again in the neck as they swam for
freedom. Noose was also shot in the back
but managed to survive. She watched her
husband die and sink to the bottom of the
ocean. The men that shot them left her for
dead as they couldn't see through the blood
in the water and so she swam underneath
them all to one of their smaller boats,
stabbed and strangled the two men guarding
it to death with the rope that was still
around her neck, and sailed off into the
sunset to find herself a home here with us.
The hanging damaged her voice so she
doesn't say a lot, but I can assure you
Tobias that for the right guy she has one
hell of a mouth!"
Noose smiles and whispers into Tobias's ear,
"You are the right man."
Tobias squeezes her close to him and
whispers back, "If only I could steal a boat
right now and take you away to our own
little island."
A warm, ephemeral moment falls upon the
group as a loving spark between Tobias and

Noose rekindles a feeling of hopeful romance, like a blossoming bud growing through charred remains of a forest fire. Maggie interrupts the tranquility as she charges over to start clearing away the drinks, "Come on girls! Blackbeard will be here soon. Make yourself scarce and try not to cause too much trouble. Jack, Tobias, I need you both to come sit over by the bar. If anything kicks off I need you close to the weapons otherwise we won't stand a chance against their crew. I've heard Blackbeard is a reasonable man and keeps his men in check so we should be ok."

Chapter 8

A Night To Remember

lackbeard's men
flood through
the entrance in
a boisterous
manner; some
shouting and
singing whilst
others play-fight
or race to a
table to win a
seat first. Only
a few remain calm and collected as they
scout out the area for their King. They
observe the area around the bar whilst
securing a suitable table for Blackbeard and
once settled, two of the high-ranking
crewmembers split up; one makes his way to
the door and the other strolls assuredly over
to where Jack and Tobias are sitting. He
drags a chair across to their table, sits down
with them and calls over to Maggie who is
already getting the glasses ready, "Get me
and my new friends a round of your finest
drink please." Then he places his weapons

on the table and eyes up the pair with a wicked grin, "The name's Caesar. You part of this establishment or just hoping to shake hands with the greatest pirate that ever lived?"

Tobias decides to welcome the pirate's questions with humour, "Maybe it is you that has just met the greatest pirate duo of all time. Our master plan is to rob you all of your treasures and get you incredibly drunk in the process."

Caesar bursts out laughing and shakes their hands, "I like you two. I promise we won't cause much trouble." He glances over at the entrance and bows his head to signal his leader. They too are drawn to where the Pirate King is standing menacingly in the doorway; his hand runs through his huge black beard before he removes his hat briefly as he lifts off his shoulder holster and then dusts his dark blue coat before being escorted to his seat. His heavy, leather boots thump loudly over the bustling atmosphere as he parts a way through his followers. Caesar takes his drink and gets ready to join his captain, "All is good my friends. He likes the place. I'll put in a good word for you."

Before he leaves the table, Jack has a few enquires to make, "Ceasar, have you ever heard of a man called Jonathan Brook?"

"No, sorry kid. Who is he?" Caesar asks.

"He's my stepfather. I'm trying to find him and my real father." Jack replies a little disheartened.

"Fuck. That's a lot of fathers to find. Mine was a chieftain back in Africa, but he died when I was young from fever and then I took his place. I'll ask around and see if anybody knows Jonathan Brook. I'd better get back to Thatche or he'll think I'm forming a mutiny!" Caesar smirks and leans in to shake their hands again.

"Thatche?" Tobias quizzes.

"Yeah. Edward Thatche. Blackbeard. See you boys later." He answers and shouts to his crew as he leaves Jack and Tobias, "Who's ready to lose some coin?"

Jack tries to get a glimpse of the mighty Pirate King, but being enclosed in a dark corner of the room by his rowdy entourage and still wearing his large, black hat that casts a shadow over his face, Jack is unable to see him properly. The gloomy resemblance is more fitting to the Grim Reaper than just a mere mortal man.

Tobias hits Jack on the arm to warn him, "Jack! Cut it out. If he gets suspicious because you keep eyeballing them we won't be leaving this place alive."

"Sorry. There's something about him that draws me in." Jack admits and turns focus to his drink.

"You'd better not leave me here so you can go join Blackbeard's crew! They'll have you scrubbing the deck with a rat carcass." Tobias laughs and tips some of his drink into Jack's, "Here you go, you need it more than me."

"You're an arsehole Tobias, but I wouldn't have you any other way!" Jack responds as he raises his glass to his friend, "Brothers!" Tobias lifts his to meet instantly, "Brothers to the end!"

The evening remains relatively quiet as the pirates keep themselves occupied under the close watch of their captain, with only one incident involving a flintlock being raised and fired up into the roof after losing doubloons in a dice game, which was then met by one of Blackbeard's right hand men punching the raucous man unconscious and propping him back in his chair to sleep it off. Then apart from occasionally shouting over for more drinks and flirting with Maggie when she delivered them, they are more captivated by the discussions and planning of their next big robbery than anything else the place has to offer. The ideas range from petty thievery to taking down the British Empire with a pirate armada.

Blackbeard has very little involvement in his crew's philosophies and instead he talks privately with Caesar and a few others sat at his table. That is until their entire evening comes to a sudden end as an exhausted young pirate crashes through the door trying to catch his breath.

Caesar jumps up from his chair as everybody else falls silent and turns to see what the commotion is about, "Why the fuck have you left the ship? What are the others doing?"

The boy stutters his words as he is struck in the limelight, "They are still on the ship⸺ Stede Bonnet has just told us⸺ On the Adventure⸺"

Caesar interrupts him, "We know who Stede Bonnet is you idiot!! What has he said? Spit it out boy!"

"There's a couple of merchant ships on their way to Carolina from Madeira again. Apparently they've been told to go a different way after the last times we've hit them which has actually put them on a route not far from here. They'll have soldiers onboard this time. There's a shit load of wine and sugar though." The boy blurts out excitedly.

All heads turn towards their leader, who holds them in wild anticipation as he finishes his beverage slowly, wipes his beard with his jacket sleeve, stands up and takes his shoulder holster from the chair, puts it on and adjusts his firearms and sword before raising his head to announce his verdict to the eager crowd before him like a judge in a courtroom. Fingertips tap anxiously and others lift themselves to the edge of their seats as the cohorts struggle to contain themselves before the sentence is determined. Finally, Blackbeard breaks a devilish smile and makes his declaration, "I don't know about you lot, but I am rather in need of some Madeira wine as we are a little too light on barrels for my liking!"

The room explodes in a volcanic display of scandalous delight as the pirate horde bundle out of the tavern and race back to their ship.

Maggie leans over the bar to speak to Jack and Tobias, "I've got to pop out to meet my friend who sent the note before. I won't be long."

"Do you want us to come with you?" Tobias asks her.

"No, it's ok. We meet every week like this." Maggie states and looks over at the departing buccaneers. "Jack, I think now would be a good chance to speak to Blackbeard. Also, when I get back, I found something in Carl's desk in the office you will really want to see."

"Good idea. Thanks Maggie, I'll have a look with you after. Right, let's see how this pans out now he isn't swamped with protection. Hopefully Caesar will help me out." Jack proclaims as he leaves the table and hurries to catch Blackbeard before it is too late.

The Pirate King is already by the exit when Jack is about to reach him, although he is stopped in his tracks by the end of a pistol aimed at his head. "Turn around before I blow a hole through your other eye." One of Blackbeard's bodyguards snarls hostilely.

Blackbeard pauses and looks over his shoulder at Jack. The fabricated myths of him being the devil himself and a stone-cold killer filled with pure evil and violence somehow fall unfittingly on this man; the famous black beard and long, dark, sun-bleached hair that hangs disheveled from under his hat as it covers his weathered, ageing face from a lifetime at sea. A strange connection sends shivers down Jack's spine as the infamous pirate stares directly into his soul with inquisitive, gentle eyes before disappearing into the night.

Ceasar slaps the other man's pistol out of Jack's direction, "Israel, leave him be. This kid's ok. Get back to the ship, I'll settle up here." Israel holsters his weapon and leaves without any complaint. Caesar places a heavy coin purse and letter into Jack's hands. "At least you can now say you've come face to face with the notorious Israel Hands and survived." He chuckles, then points to the items he gave Jack, "That'll cover the drinks, any damages we made and a little extra from the captain to say thank you. Now, I wish you the best of luck finding your fathers, Brook, and I hope our paths cross again in the future."

They shake hands and Jack says his goodbye whilst holding his grip firmly, "I hope so too Caesar. Where will you be heading to next?"

"After we get our wine we'll be heading back to Carolina to get ourselves a pardon for our crimes so we can get the heat off of us for a bit. Maybe you two can come join us when you're done here." Caesar lets go

and joins his felonious family for their next
adventure.
Jack returns to an impatient Tobias and
shows him the weighty bag of coins,
"Maggie has enough coin here to retire on
and we have an invite to Carolina when we
want to join their crew."
"Sounds perfect. Might have to see if I can
bring Noose with me though." He smiles
and winks to Jack, then notices the other
item in his hand, "What's that?"
Jack hands it to Tobias, "It's from
Blackbeard. Have a read whilst I go put
this in Maggie's office and see what she
wanted me to look at."

Upon the desk is a small diary, battered
and beaten with some pages stained from
blood and seawater. Maggie has left a note
tucked between a couple of pages, so Jack
opens the page and reads the note marking
where to look;

Jack...

This was Carl's book he had
with him during the war. I know
it may be difficult to read and
isn't the outcome you wanted but
at least now you know.

See you later,

Love Maggie x

Jack begins to read from Carl's diary and the story has a strange similarity to how Jack and Tobias ended up floating across the sea;

We were carrying out our patrolling duties as normal when we came across three Spanish ships. No retreat. No escape. The bumbling idiot on the other ship paniched and steered straight into their line of fire. All of them dead instantly. Left us to fight by ourselves. Captain gave a great speech. Felt like I could take on a hundred men with just my sword. Then it all went to shit.

Captain and half the crew killed by cannon fire. Brook stepped up. Never really got time to speak to the guy. He was quiet and just got on with stuff. Didn't think he had it in him. Turned the ship out of fire and they chased us for such a long time. Brook grounded the ship half full of water and we stood our ground. Poor guy took a hell of a lot of injuries but took down at least six or seven with his sword. Only four of us left. Carried Brook for miles but didn't make it. He was

talking in my ear the whole
time. Only words I could
remember were the names
Abigail and Jack. Repeated
them over and over like a
mad man. Didn't think
he'd die though. Goddamn
hero. Saved our lives. I
never even drew my sword.
Feel like it should have
been me. Gave him a proper
hero's burial. Have no idea
where it was now but he's
in a better place. Hope he
finds his family in the
afterlife. Rest in peace
Jonathan Brook....

The hollow space feels even emptier and lonelier as it fills with crippling failure and bitter veracity. The thought of not being able to see his stepfather again leaves a painful burden of an unfinished story. He loses composure, embraces Carl's diary and sobs as the fate of Jonathan Brook burns freshly in his mind.

"Jack, you ok?" A soft, sensitive voice asks from the doorway.

Jack wipes his eyes and looks around to see who is there, "Aphrodite. Sorry, I didn't know you were there." He turns away to hide his face.

Aphrodite shuts the door to the office, moves closer to Jack and puts her arms around him, "Why are you apologising for? You're allowed to have feelings Jack." She leans against the desk and takes hold of Jack's arms to move him to face her and then holds his hands tenderly. "I'll let you in on a little secret but then you have to tell me yours after. Deal?"

"I like your bargaining skills. What's the secret?" Jack quizzes.

"Well, there's more than just one actually—First one, my real name is Phoebe. Second one is that I have a feeling deep down that you might be the one to fill my lonely heart. The last one, Noose wants us all to move to an island together where her and Tobias can live forever together. Your friend must have quite the silver tongue to win her over so soon."

"Phoebe. That's a beautiful name for a goddess of love. And you haven't seen what my tongue can do yet. Also, I thought you were only interested in pirate captains?" He grins as his flirting makes Phoebe giggle.

"Well, I can make an exception this time. But who says you won't be the next Pirate King of the Caribbean?" Phoebe states with eyes full of lustful craving as she bites her lip seductively at the thought of what is on her mind to say to Jack next. "I'm kind of curious to find out what your tongue can do though."

Without saying a word more, Jack runs his hand through her silky, golden locks, making her close her eyes and inhale with aching desire as his fingertips caress the back of her head, then he pulls her in gently until her lips are touching his. An ember of wishful affection intensifies into a raging fire of yearning covetousness. Jack slides down her underwear to her feet and lifts her onto the desk, then he kisses her neck and runs his hands up her thighs as he makes his way down to find a buried treasure that no Pirate King could ever part with once in his possession.

She climbs off of Jack and they both lie together on the office floor panting and sweaty. "Wow! That was amazing! Think I'm starting to like this secluded island idea with you more and more."
Jack moves his arm underneath Phoebe as she rests her head on his chest and they hold each other in a moment of soothing envision until Jack disrupts the dreamy illusory with his part of the deal they made, "My stepfather left for the war when I was a kid and then my mother died not long after that. I left where I came from to find my stepfather and to also find who my real father is‟ Or was. Maggie's husband left a

diary behind that revealed what happened to my stepfather."

"I'm sorry about your mother Jack. What happened to your stepfather?" Phoebe lifts her head and looks caringly into Jack's eyes.

"He saved Carl and a few others by steering their ship out of danger and fought off the enemy so they could escape, but he died as Carl carried him to safety from his wounds. I won't ever get to see him again." Jack replies forlornly.

Phoebe kisses him softly and gives her opinion to help mend the pain, "Jack, it sounds like he was a hero. He would be so proud of you being just like him and coming all this way to find him. He may not be here with you anymore but the important thing is that he is there with your mother and they can both watch over the rest of your journey together. Although they both probably just closed their eyes after what we just did." She grins and bites Jack's shoulder playfully, cracking a smile from his sad expression, "You're my brave hero Jack. Maybe I can come with you to

find your real father and one day we will
get to meet your mother and stepfather
together?"

He kisses her on the head, "I'd like that.
You know Tobias has nothing on your
silver tongue."

They laugh and Phoebe straddles him again,
"I think somebody is ready for me again?"
As she begins to tease him with her hips,
there is spine-chilling scream from outside
and the pair jump to their feet. "Stay
here." Jack orders as he leaves the office
and meets with Tobias and Noose by the
bar. Tobias throws him a pistol and they
advance tactically outside to where the
scream came from. It is almost pitch black
in the street but as their vision adapts, they
see Pearl sat on the floor with her head in
her hands. She gets up and runs to Noose
who has followed Jack and Tobias and
holds her in hysterical distress.

"Oh fuck. Jack. Fuck. No." Tobias
exclaims with a broken voice as he grabs
Jack's arm.

Frozen in horror, they look up at two
bodies hanging from posts with rope tied

around their necks. Their rescuer and new friend, Maggie, swings vacuously with hands and feet bound next to her informer.

Jack draws his sword and moves towards the posts where Maggie is attached to, "We need to cut them down Tobias. She can't be left up there any longer."

Being strung up so high leaves no easy way of cutting them down; as the blade slices through the rope below, the bodies drop with an inhumanly thud as they hit the floor underneath. Jack cuts the rope binding Maggie's limbs, then upon further examination he convulses in revulsion and throws up when he looks at her face and discovers all her teeth have been pulled out and her tongue cut from her mouth.

Tobias finds the same with the man's body, "Holy shit. They've pulled out all their teeth. What sick fuck would do that?"

"The Dentist." Jack mumbles, spitting out the remaining vomit and wiping his mouth, "The piece of shit wants to take over Maggie's business."

From the darkness surrounding the pair, a slow, single clapping noise gets louder and louder until a figure appears from cover and applauds as he enters their viewpoint. His sadistic smile glints in the moonlight as the villainous monster bares his golden identity, "Looks like you backed the wrong side boys. Let's see if you can hold out longer than that stupid old bitch did."

"I'm going to cut you into pieces!" Jack yells and rushes towards the Dentist.

"Now!!" The Dentist shouts, which is followed by a rapid downpour of musket balls.

Tobias drops his crutch and throws himself at Jack, forcing them behind an improvised shield as a fusillade of lightning gunfire scatters the wooden frame of the tipped cart and food crates that are the only line of protection from the ambushing force. Soon the firing dwindles as the attackers reload their weapons, but the pause is not just to rearm, it is to make way for a cannon to be wheeled into action as they load and aim to blast Tobias and Jack into oblivion.

Before the friends meet their maker, a single shot from the tavern roof strikes perfectly as

the bullet passes straight through the ears of
the goon about to light the cannon fuse and
the others around him flee to nearby shelter.
The next shot is another impeccable blow
to the cowering adversary as this time their
leader has left his foot a few inches out of
his hiding place and becomes a vulnerable
target for the merciless projectile as it rips
through his ankle.
He screams in agony and recoils into the
shadows, "Ahhhhhh! She's on the fucking
roof! Kill her!!"
The red-haired sniper vanishes from her
position and as the Dentist's thugs invade
vehemently, the girls have their own
ambuscade in place; loaded weapons have
already been appointed to every window and
are played seamlessly in order like a piano
recital. Each key pressed brings its
individual harmony to the composition
presented to the dazzled audience in front of
the stage.
As recently departed cadavers decorate the
streets with blood, the lasting fighters follow
their pusillanimous superior as he withdraws,

leaving his men behind with no order of retreat.

Tobias and Jack draw their swords and enter the silent fog to finish off any remaining foes that escaped the girl's onslaught. Out of half a dozen fallen fatalities, only one man is left barely alive as he coughs up the only air left in his lungs. Tobias steps on the man's injury and kneels down close to him, "Where is he going to be hiding?"

"Warehouse~ Docks." The man splutters as he drifts into the underworld as Tobias removes his boot.

The girls gather outside and together with Jack and Tobias they tearfully carry Maggie and her friend through the smoky battlefield and into the tavern so they can prepare them for a proper send off and burial.

Drinks are lined around her covered body on the table and Phoenix lifts her glass first and delivers a speech through crushing grief, "To Maggie. Our mother. Our best friend.

We will avenge your death. May you find happiness with Carl again. We love you Maggie."

"To Maggie." Echoes through the room as revenge sits heavy on their minds.

Chapter 9

Eye For An Eye, Tooth For A Tooth

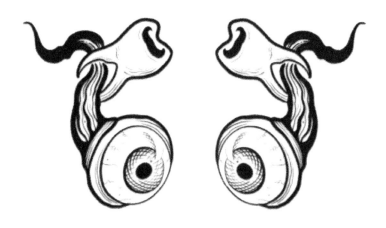

184

he smell of blood and gunpowder still lingers freshly as it sits amongst an eerie smokescreen that hides the collateral repercussion of man's violent tenacity for gluttonous power. The sun is still in hiding but releases a scintilla of early morning light as it peeks with mere existence through the greyed obscurity that blemishes the remnants of nightfall.

Phoenix leads the group with an implacable thirst for brutal retribution. Holding her rifle close to her chest, she strides through the desolate streets in hopeful anticipation of finding her first target.

The rest trail behind in complete silence as they await the unexpected. All of them are

armed to their teeth with an unremitting
supply of weapons; Pearl is strapped from
head to toe in knives, Phoebe carries two
flintlocks and has her sword by her side
ready to unsheathe, Noose prefers more
intimate combat and plans to deal death
from the shadows with her rope and blades,
Tobias stays close to Noose with cutlass
already drawn like a rhinoceros bowing its
horn and trampling the ground, ready to
charge to protect its loved ones at any cost.
Aside from what he is wielding, he is loaded
with multiple rifles upon his back and bags
of ammo tied to his belt despite still having
to support himself with his crutch.
Jack keeps to the front with Phoenix and
watches carefully as he figures out a plan of
action for their assault or if they run into
another trap along the way.

They approach the warehouse and Jack
directs Phoenix and the others to cover so
they can assess the area and devise a scheme
that does not involve a suicidal foray.
Their headquarters is abnormally quiet and
unguarded, which worries Jack as he starts

to wonder whether the Dentist has foreseen an immediate counterattack and laid down a deceiving plot.

After examining their surroundings, Jack verbalises his method of incursion, "They must be expecting us. We need to draw the henchmen out of hiding whilst some of us get in position to penetrate the heart of their operation as stealthily as possible when they're distracted by the frontal attack. We leave no prisoners and not a single one of them can escape into the trees behind." He points to a few nearby houses and requests Phoenix's skills, "Reckon you can climb up onto one of those and work your magic? It's a good vantage point to cut off any retreat from behind and pick off the bastards cowering behind cover out the front."

"It would be my pleasure." Phoenix answers valiantly and then addresses the other girls, "If you need help, raise your hand to me and I'll kill anyone in your way. Jack is right with being smart about this; I don't want all of this to be for nothing. This is our island now."

"Where do you need me to go Jack?" Tobias asks.

"I need you at the front of the building to scare the living shit out of them. Keep your eye on Phoenix as she will signal when to fire once I have given her a sign that everybody is in place." He turns to the girls who are keen to carry out their orders, "Phoebe, you're with Tobias. Make sure when one of you is reloading that the other one is shooting so they can't advance. And move cover so they don't get a fixed position on you both. Pearl, Noose, you're with me; I need your expertise with close combat. We will be sneaking around the back of the building and as soon as they move to fight Tobias and Phoebe, we will kill all who's heads are turned. I will make sure their leader is kept out of the conflict. Without him, they will crumble and lose any formation like a bunch of headless chickens. So, are we ready to destroy these vermin?"

"Yes!" They all agree and disperse in various directions to carry out their selected duties.

Through the small cracks in the wooden warehouse structure, Jack peeks through the eyeholes to get an idea of the layout and to make sure the enemy are actually inside. To his amazement, the Dentist and his subordinates are in no defensive state or even ready for any sort of combat. Their egocentric commander limps around their lair with drink in hand and mouthful of purloined treasure as he grins from ear to ear in confident success. His men join him in disillusioned victory as they celebrate in a state of incredulity to any possible reprisal after their cowardly retreat merely a couple of hours ago. There are only five of them left, with two less functioning fighters writhing in pain in the corner as their medic tries to keep them alive.

Idiocy has altered the mission in Jack's favour and with diminutive resistance he decides to concoct another tactic. He crouches down with Pearl and Noose and whispers the updated idea, "Those imbeciles are in there getting pissed. There are only about five or six of them that can fight. I am going to go back to Tobias and get them to attack and retreat rather than drawing them out. I think they are going to anchor down and hold their position being so few of them. Stay here and watch the exits in case any of them decide to leave. I'll be right back." The girls accept the plan and Jack scurries to the front of the building where he finds Tobias and Phoebe concealed in the middle of a stack of cargo crates.

"What's going on?" Phoebe asks with concern.

"They're in there drinking and having a great time. I don't think drawing them out here will work. The doors at the front are open so move in close, ready yourselves with multiple weapons and when Phoenix gives you the signal, open fire at them and then retreat to your original positions to reload and let us hit them from behind. Agreed?"

"Got it." Phoebe replies.

"I like this plan!" Tobias beams and starts loading another flintlock.

Jack is about to return but Phoebe grabs his arm and kisses him intensely before letting him go. "Be careful Jack, I want you in one piece."

"You too my goddess. Look after Tobias for me, he has a gift for getting shot in every fight." Jack struggles to let go of his newfound love but he must get back to the other two.

With everybody now back in position, Jack signals to Phoenix who adjusts her aim and then waves her arm for Tobias and Phoebe to begin.

Jack envisions the pair moving towards the doors and times it in his head to when the gunshots should go off— Nothing happens. Silence.

Maybe something has gone wrong. Maybe it was all an illusion to fool them into another forbidding ensnarement. "*Has something happened to them?*" Jack's thoughts play unnerving games in his mind.

He moves to see what is happening and checks through the gaps again, but in that split moment his face touches the wood, all hell breaks loose; his friends burst open the doors fully and the deafening booms reverberate around the building as every musket ball pierces flesh and bone of the befuddled adversaries.

One of the shots blows a hole straight through the bottom of a metal tankard and embeds itself into the brain of the man drinking from it. Another ruptures the jugular of an unsuspecting victim as he applies a bandage to his arm. The rest find a leg or arm of the recoiling deserters. Before they get a chance to fight back, Tobias and Phoebe are long gone and the next stage has already commenced as the beautiful assassins disappear from Jack's side, enter the vicinity and are already wreaking devastation upon the survivors. Like ghosts haunting the living, they do not make a sound as their lethal metal sends the enemy boarding the everlasting boat to the netherworlds.

Jack rushes in to find the Dentist, however, is caught under fire immediately as he enters; his target takes a shaky shot at him whilst scrambling up a ladder to the upper floor and throws his weapon in anger as the bullet skims past Jack's head and hits the door frame behind.

Jack follows but judiciously chooses another route up a foundation beam as he knows he will be met with a sword or a bullet to the head as he reaches the top step. He climbs over the railing on to the floor above and ducks behind a hoard of storage boxes before moving charily to the other side where he last saw the recreant. The building becomes uncomfortably silent and only the creaking of floorboards and old rafters spoil the ethereal ambiance as Jack's boots unsettle the resting edifice.

As he turns the corner, an open pulley hatch at the end lights up the dingy passageway but there is still no sign of the Dentist.

"Come out and fight me like a man! Or did you lose your balls in the fight?" Jack calls out as he draws his sword and awaits his opponent's response.

A cloud of dust puffs into the air as a shuffling figure arises from his refuge with quivering steel in his hand, "Even if I die here today, I'll take you along with me."

The Dentist defies his injury and charges towards Jack as the reoccurring memories of Nathaniel's training gyrate through his mind, "*Don't lose concentration. It's not about how hard you can hit, it's all about the timing and a well-placed attack.*" The words of his mentor resonate as he matches the belligerent challenger and deflects a heavy downward strike, parrying another off-balance slash as the Dentist slams into an overhanging joist.

"I'm going to enjoy ripping out your teeth as you're bleeding to death from my sword." The Dentist yells before storming Jack again.

This time, Jack dodges a swing at his head although he is knocked to the floor and loses his weapon as he nearly falls out of the hatch. The Dentist thrusts his sword at Jack's neck and gets it stuck as he narrowly misses. Jack uses the opportunity to kick directly into his enemy's knee and the disabling blow crunches the bone as he forces it in the wrong direction.

The Dentist shrieks in excruciation, "I'm going to kill you!!" He crawls onto Jack

194

and grabs him by the throat. Jack tries to reach for his dagger attached to his waist, but as soon as he releases his arm the weight of the attacking force nearly crushes his neck completely, so he grabs hold of the Dentist's arms again to relieve a tiny bit of pressure.

Scanning for a lifeline, he notices through the reflection of the wedged sword Phoenix running along the roof of one of the opposite buildings, so he pushes his legs up into the Dentist's chest to raise him higher and forces his chin up with one his hands, but his hold abates as the choke gets stronger and the unendurable pressure pulls Jack into looming insentience.

Before Jack enters unconsciousness, a muffled bang sounds from a distance and within milliseconds a hole appears in the Dentist's head. His grip loosens as blood oozes from his wound and his eyes wane into extinction. Jack frees the stiff fingers around his neck, lifts the body off of him and locates his sword before dragging his nemesis's corpse to the edge and rolls him out of the hatch and onto the crates below to display their victory.

"Jack! Are you hurt?" Phoebe asks from the top of the ladder as she finds him covered in blood and lying on his back on the floor.

Jack sits up and laughs, "If you think this is bad, you should see the other guy." He moves closer and embraces Phoebe. "Things may have gone very differently if it wasn't thanks to Phoenix's rifle. Are the others ok? Please don't tell me Tobias has been shot again!"

Phoebe giggles and kisses him. "Everyone is ok. Tobias actually didn't get shot, although he did fall over his crutch when we retreated and spent most of his time cursing as he reloaded."

Jack is tickled by the thought of his friend's misfortune but is glad that he was not hurt in the fight. "What about Pearl and Noose?"

"They are fine. Pearl was grazed by a stray shot but apart from that they enjoyed butchering the guys downstairs. Noose is

now stuck to Tobias again and Pearl is
with Phoenix outside." She replies and kisses
Jack again, "Are you ready to come down
and celebrate?"

"After you. I get to take in the best view
of the island from here." He says flirtingly
as Phoebe positions herself on the ladder and
exposes her cleavage to him.

"Fancy exploring the mountains quickly?"
She dismounts the ladder again and places
his hand into her undergarments, "Or
maybe it's not just the mountains that you
want?"

Chapter 10

Like Father, Like Son

hoenix is standing over the body of the Dentist like a vulture picking at the remains of a rotting animal as she starts to rip out his gold teeth and stores them in a coin purse. She glances over at Jack and Phoebe as they leave the warehouse to join their team, "It's very rare to find a man that likes to take his time. However, some men I am more than happy to collect their coin when they can't even last past me touching their trousers!" She chortles as she yanks the last tooth free, "Last one! Can't have him making any bargains with the Devil if he arrives in Hell with a mouth full of gold can we now. Plus, the town needs it more than he does." Placing the last tooth in her possession, she

leaves the body to shake Jack's hand, "Thank you Jack. You and Tobias helped save this place and avenge Maggie."

"It is I that owes you a great deal of gratitude after your skills saved my life up there." Jack shakes her hand and hugs her before they let go for a more serious conversation, "So what happens next?"

"Well, I'm guessing you'll be wanting to carry on with your journey?" She enquires.

"Yes. But once I find what I am looking for I can come back if you have a place for us again." He says lightheartedly.

"Of course. I'll make sure you only have pay a little bit for protection." She walks Jack to face the warehouse dock and points out a small ship harboured there, "That was the Dentist's. It's yours now. I know I joke, but you know you're always welcome back here Jack. I understand you must fulfill your destiny first though. We will take over the whole operation here and do Maggie proud." She slaps him on the back and makes her way to the warehouse entrance where Pearl is searching the dead for anything of any value. "I think you have Phoebe and Tobias craving your attention now."

Jack returns to his lover's arms as she is discussing something with Tobias and Noose. She grasps him in excitement, "They're going to get married!!"

"That's great news! She'll make an honest man of you yet Tobias!" Jack jests as he hugs the enamored twosome. "I guess we should help Phoenix and Pearl clear up the place and then get you two over to the church before we set sail for Carolina."

The ceremony is soon underway once the group have cleared their former competitors from the killing grounds, reaped the spoils of war and taken control of all the newly acquired sites of business. The other townsfolk are unhesitant to become abiding aficionadas as they ally with the new head of their hometown confederacy by aiding Phoenix with the removal and desecration of the Dentist's gang of corpses. They are slung into a shallow grave and set alight, apart from the Dentist who has his body hung by his neck and tied to a tree branch

dangling over the bay by the docks to warn
any visiting guests.
The rest of the residents help out preparing
for the grand wedding; they disseminate in
every direction to collect decorative
arrangements and marriage embellishments
like bowerbirds building a display court,
filled with conspicuous objects to secure the
prenuptial courtship before the marital
enactment initiates.

Tobias arrives at the altar with Jack in
jury-rigged formal jackets, trousers and shoes
burnished to make audiences' eyes squint.
Jack takes Tobias's crutch so he can stand
stalwartly and wait for his fiancée to
accompany him for their matrimony.
The girls are soon to enter and draw every
head in the church as they glide down the
aisle with their glamorous dresses and
breathtaking beauty.
Noose struggles to hold back her tears as
she joins her love and they both hold hands
as they declaim an emotional reading.
A ritual of true happiness and a missing
link chained back together as two lives that

have lived through misery and destruction
have at last found peace within the world
they have endured so far and discovered
hopefulness in nurturing a bourgeoning love
through the scars and remorseless grief that
once held them down.

After the proceedings, the girls take Noose
back to the bar and Tobias follows Jack to
the docks where they board their ship and
look out over the horizon.
"Is this where we part ways my brother? I
know you want your island with Noose and
I think you may have had enough of
catching bullets for me." Jack insists with a
heavy heart.
Tobias puts his arm around Jack and hands
him the note Blackbeard left behind, "I
made a promise to you Jack. Noose and I
both agree we need a proper adventure
together before retiring to our island."

Jack opens up the folded paper and reads
the message;

Thank you for your hospitality. May the stolen riches of the wealthy beasts see you prosper. Never surrender to the oppressing tyranny that enslaves us. Live free or die trying.

E.T.

Jack recalls the letter given to his mother by his father that he put in his naval jacket pocket before leaving. Even though it is now lost, the handwriting is imprinted in his mind. This particular handwriting matches that of the note left for Maggie with faultless comparison. His father's initials E.T. stand for Edward Thatche---Blackbeard---

Meanwhile

◆ ◆ ◆

Soon after arriving just off of Charles Town, South Carolina, Blackbeard finds himself in dire need of medical treatment and payment for his crew. He must carry out another infamous feat before tracking down the right man in power to issue a pardon for his offenses, only then can he withdraw to a more settled existence away from the law and bounty hunters.

Forming a blockade at the Charles Town Port with his ships, he plunders any vessel attempting to leave or enter, robbing them of all supplies and specie and taking their captains as hostages to bargain for his demands.

A parlay group were sent to meet with Governor Robert Johnson and his council with one of the prisoners as leverage, who relayed the requests to them. All Blackbeard wanted from Charles Town was a chest of medicine and then for his men to walk free. If this was not met then they would murder all the captives, send their heads to Governor Johnson and set all ships on fire that they had commandeered.

Despite the resistance, Charles Town had already suffered enough from expensive battling with natives and recent pirate exploits from the notorious pirate captain, Charles Vane, and so were in no condition to fight Blackbeard. They were also missing a fellow councilman who was now in the hands of the Pirate King, which swayed the decision in favour of agreeing to their demands.

The pirates returned safely to their ships with the extremely precious chest full of medicine. After almost a week, Blackbeard released all hostages and seized ships and left for Fish Town in Topsail.

He then guided his Fleet into Topsail Inlet, with the *Revenge* and other sloops going first. But disaster struck as his prized ship *Queen Anne's Revenge* smashed into the sandbar at shallow waters under full sail. They tried desperately to free the ship but only damaged it further and sank one of the smaller sloops in the process.

Blackbeard decides to send away the captain of the *Revenge,* Steed Bonnet to get more help to offload their treasures. Although, after splitting up the crew and sending away those he did not trust as much, he jumps aboard one of the other sloops and maroons most of the remaining crew on the nearby sand banks as he disappears with his closest crewmen and all the important contents of his abandoned ship.

Crammed aboard their small Spanish-built sloop, Blackbeard and his new crew head for their final sanctuary. A tiny hamlet of Bath, a newly formed settlement comprising of fewer than two dozen homes and approximately around a hundred residents living there. It is the capital of North Carolina and where Governor Charles Eden is living amongst its inhabitants.

The pirates use their bargaining skills yet again and in return for their protection, wealth and to help Bath thrive as a colony, they are to be granted a pardon and allowed to settle there﹍

The Story Continues...

As Jack, Tobias, Phoebe and Noose leave behind the place that gave them all another chance in life, they dream of one day returning to their paradise after Jack has found his father.

The sea has remained calm for the first part of their journey but after getting too relaxed and accustomed to the serene settings, a brief lapse in concentration befalls them as up ahead storm clouds spawn in the distance and shadowing behind them are a small fleet of ships.

Who are these impending pursuers?

Will their new ship continue to survive the treacherous seas ahead of them?

Will Blackbeard get his pardon before Jack gets to him?

Volume 2

The

Pirate

Prince

Printed in Great Britain
by Amazon